THE PRINCE

Hushang Golshiri

The Prince

TRANSLATED
FROM THE PERSIAN
BY

James Buchan

Harvill Secker
LONDON

Published by Harvill Secker, 2005

2 4 6 8 10 9 7 5 3 1

First published with the title *Shazdeh Ehtejab*
by Zaman Publishing House, Tehran, 1969

First published in Great Britain in 2005 by
HARVILL SECKER
Random House, 20 Vauxhall Bridge Road
London SW1V 2SA

Random House Australia (Pty) Limited
20 Alfred Street, Milsons Point, Sydney,
New South Wales 2061, Australia

Random House New Zealand Limited
18 Poland Road, Glenfield,
Auckland 10, New Zealand

Random House South Africa (Pty) Limited
Isle of Houghton, Corner of Boundary Road & Carse O'Gowrie,
Houghton 2198, South Africa

The Random House Group Limited Reg. No. 954009
www.randomhouse.co.uk

A CIP catalogue record for this book is available from the British Library

ISBN 1 84343 171 8

Papers used by Random House are natural, recyclable products made
from wood grown in sustainable forests; the manufacturing processes conform to the
environmental regulations of the country of origin

Typeset in Adobe Jenson
by SX Composing DTP, Rayleigh, Essex
Printed and bound in Great Britain by
William Clowes Ltd, Beccles, Suffolk

INTRODUCTION

James Buchan

Pasha o pasheh hameja hastand.
Princes and flies – you can't get away from them.

PERSIAN PROVERB

The Prince, Shazdeh Ehtejab in Persian, came out in Tehran in the spring of 1969 and was soon spoken of as a masterpiece. It showed that Iranian writers had learned the techniques of European and American modern fiction and added some tricks of their own. In treating the grand themes of Iranian history as wistful and shabby household drama, Hushang Golshiri had no right to succeed and succeeded.

The Prince tells the story, as Golshiri once said in one of those Delphic interviews so beloved of the Iranian modernists, 'of a chap who had a cough and

I

died'.* The narrative unfolds in a single night in a provincial Persian town in the first half of the twentieth century.

Prince Khosrow Ehtejab, one of the last survivors of a royal family that has been dethroned, returning home at sundown runs into Murad, the old family coachman crippled in a carriage accident. Murad has the habit of calling on him to announce the death of someone or other and pick up a tip. The Prince's wife, a paternal cousin called Fakhronissa – 'Pride of Womanhood' in the elaborate nomenclature of aristocratic Iran – has already fallen prey to consumption. Even before her death, the Prince had taken up with her maid Fakhri – 'Pridey' – in a rambling house that is being voided of everything of value.

Unperturbed, the Prince tips the old coachman and climbs up to his empty room. As he coughs his lungs out, his mind strays over the mementoes of his family's lost power and prosperity, objects and photographs and lithographed books of memoirs. Scenes of feudal violence and arbitrary cruelty play out amid a quarter-Europeanised domesticity. All the while, the pallid image of Fakhronissa flickers at the edge of view,

* *Hamrah ba Shazdeh Ehtejab*, ed F. Taheri and A. Azimi, Tehran, 1380 (2001), p33.

taunting the Prince with his impotence and degeneracy.

The Prince has tried to make of Fakhri a sort of simulacrum of her mistress, a Fakhronissa that neither coughs blood nor answers back. The girl sits down to dinner as Fakhronissa, then puts on her headscarf and washes it up as Fakhri. Yet her own nature will out. She is plump and sexy, where Fakhronissa was pale and frigid, she bursts out of her mistress's dresses, cackles when pinched, smells of soap and lye. Every embrace ends in slaps and tears, as every recollection leads into a *cul-de-sac* of bewilderment and disgust. The book ends just before dawn, with Murad being carried up the stairs in his wheelchair to announce, like the angel of doom Ezrail in the Koran, the death of a certain Prince Ehtejab:

'Ehtejab?'

'I mean Khosrow, who as a boy used to stand on ceremonial days beside the Great Prince who would pass a hand over his hair and say: "My boy, don't turn out a pimp like your father".'

'Aha,' said the Prince.

'He had T.B., was thin as a spindle, you couldn't recognise him. May God have mercy on him.'

The Pahlavi monarchy (1925–79), in its headlong rush to modernise Iran, did not at first recognise itself in Golshiri's feckless and poverty-stricken princelings. Bahman Farmanara's film of 1974 ('Shazdeh Ehtejab'), with Jamshid Mashayekhi as the Prince and the beautiful Fakhri Khorvash, was a more explicit insult to the institution of monarchy. Just after filming was complete and, as it were, to be on the safe side, Golshiri was jailed for six months.

The Islamic Revolution which overthrew the monarchy in 1979 had no more time than the Pahlavis for independent writers. *The Prince* offended against a new orthodoxy in matters of religion and the duties of women. Under the Islamic Republic, Golshiri was harried on every side and, for a period in the late 1990s, he was in unremitting danger of assassination. In reality, Golshiri's loyalty was to literature rather than to any programme of political reform or reaction.

The pioneering prose writers in the Iran of the twentieth century were of distinguished families. The stupendously long-lived Sayyid Mohammed Ali Jamalzadeh (c.1895–1997) was born the son of a well-known liberal cleric in Iran's second city of Isfahan, while the forebears of Sadeq Hedayat (1903–51) had furnished the Qajars with Court secretaries and ministers for three generations. In contrast, Golshiri was proud of modest origins. 'When *Shazdeh Ehtejab* was written,' Golshiri said, 'I'd never seen princes even from afar.'*

Golshiri was born in 1937 into a large Isfahanian family of small means. He grew up in the oil town of Abadan in the hot south of Iran, where his father worked as a clerk for the Anglo-Iranian Oil Company. In 1955 Hushang returned to live in Isfahan, still scattered with the elegant and fragile monuments of its glory days in the seventeenth century. He completed a bachelor's degree in Persian at Isfahan University and taught elementary and high school in the city and other towns in the oasis. In the political turmoil of the early 1960s, while Shah Mohammed Reza Pahlavi consolidated his autocratic rule, Golshiri was briefly imprisoned.

He began submitting short stories to the literary magazines at the end of the 1950s, and together with a tight circle of Isfahan writers established *Jong-e esfahan* ('The Isfahan Review'), the chief literary journal outside Tehran. Golshiri's first collection of short stories, *Mesl-e hamisheh* (*As Always*, 1968) showed the influence on his circle of the *nouveau roman* of Alain Robbe-Grillet and Claude Simon, but transferred to a

* *Hamrah ba Shazdeh Ehtejab*, p27.

provincial Persian setting. In the first story in the collection, a group of Isfahan opium addicts give the police contradictory accounts of the suicide of one of their number. It was a premonition of the hallucinatory shifts of view in *The Prince*. That year, Golshiri joined a campaign against the censorship and coercion of writers and helped establish the independent Iranian Writers' Association.

The Prince, Golshiri's first novel, appeared in the late spring of 1969. After a slow start, it was noticed in the literary journals of the capital. Farmanara's film, which together with Dariush Mehrjui's *Gav* ('Cow', 1969) established the prestige of the Persian cinema overseas, brought Golshiri an international reputation.

His next novel, *Keristin ba Kid* (*Christine and Kid*), which came out in 1971, was based in part on his love affair with a British teacher in Isfahan. It was followed by a collection of short stories called *Namazkhaneh-e kuchek-e man* (*My Little Prayer Room*, 1975), and the 1977 novel *Barreh-e gomshodeh-e rai* (*The Shepherd and the Lost Lamb*).

In the Revolution year of 1979, Golshiri married the critic and translator Farzaneh Taheri who became a close literary collaborator. As the new regime added layers of social censorship to the old political restrictions of the monarchy, the Golshiri house became a centre for both the study and teaching of literature. Golshiri continued with great difficulty to publish his novels and stories: *Masum-e panjom* (*The Fifth Innocent*, 1980), *Jobbehkhaneh* (*The Arsenal*, 1983), *Hadis-e mahigir va div* (*The Story of the Fisherman and the Demon*, 1984), and *Panj ganj* (*Five Treasures*, 1989). Sign of the times, the last was printed in Stockholm. In 1990, Golshiri sent out in separate packets to Abbas Milani in San Francisco an anonymous novel, set in Evin Prison in north Tehran during the Revolutionary Terror of the early 1980s, and translated into English by Milani as *King of the Benighted*.

In the 1990s, Golshiri all but gave up publishing to concentrate on a campaign, in the words of the 1994 Declaration of Iranian Writers, 'to remove barriers to freedom of thought and expression'. Golshiri was insulted on state television while the right-wing newspapers insinuated that he had contact with foreign powers. His final novel, *Jenn nameh* (*The Book of the Jinn*), published in Stockholm in 1998, appeared in the midst of a wave of assassinations of secular intellectuals. Among the victims were the writers Mohammed Mokhtari, Mohammed Jaafar Puyandeh and Majid Sharif. The work of Intelligence Ministry

7

agents,* the so-called 'chain murders' outraged Iranian opinion. Golshiri's speech at Mokhtari's funeral on December 15, 1998, broadcast by the Persian service of the BBC all over Iran and to the exiles, was an act of defiance to a chaotic regime and a reinforcement to the beleaguered remnants of Iranian lay society. For these acts of gallantry, Golshiri paid with his health. He died on June 5, 2000, aged sixty-three.

The dynasty of which Ehtejab is a late survivor, the Qajars, arose from the tribal wars of eighteenth-century Iran to capture the Peacock Throne in 1785. Their rule, which was by no means wholly worthless or unsuccessful, lasted until 1925 when a Cossack officer and British *protégé* named Reza Khan, who had seized power in 1921, established himself on the throne. The new dynasty, which took the ancient Persian name of Pahlavi, came to grief in the Revolution of 1979. That year the Shia clergy, which both Qajars and Pahlavis had done so much to caress and promote, declared the ancient institution of Persian monarchy to be a dead dog.

* Investigations by the Islamic Judiciary found that the murders were the work of 'rogue agents' under the direction of a senior official, Said Emami, who had just died in mysterious circumstances in prison.

The Qajar century and a half was marked by agrarian stagnation, arbitrary government, religious turmoil and persistent European infiltration. Though the founder of the dynasty, Agha Mohammed, had been castrated by his enemies, his son Fath Ali Shah made up for lost time and tissue, creating from scratch a large royal family and a permanent Court. He crammed his family quarters with women from every corner of Iran, Georgia and the Caucasus and left at his death in 1834 some sixty sons and forty daughters.

Both fascinated and alarmed by European encroachment, his successors made intermittent efforts to establish a modern administration and army. Nassereddin Shah (1831–96) – 'Great-grandfather' in this story – was so far established as to be entertained as an equal at Peterhof and Windsor Castle. He brought in shady European business interests to develop Iran's resources, but succumbed to a growing nationalism, both liberal and religious, and the assassin's bullet. The Constitutional Revolution of 1905-07, and then an unsuccessful royal *coup d'état* a year later, put an end to Qajar absolutism. Reza Khan deposed the last Qajar Shah in 1921.

These historical themes are present in the novel, but rather as shadows in the corner of the Prince's room or impressions that pass back and forth through the sieve that is his mind.

The word Qajar does not occur in *The Prince*. As for the Pahlavis, determined to rob the old Qajar aristocracy of its land and property, they are dismissed by the Prince's aunts as 'these people' (*inha*). We know we are in Isfahan because a river runs through it and on the sands the starved people drink blood from the throat of a half-dead donkey.

History moves on to no very great purpose. Turn away for a moment and you miss it: the Babi martyrs walking to their deaths in the Royal Square of Isfahan with lighted wicks inserted in their flesh, the icy asphalt on which Murad is crushed, the armoured cars and machine guns that massacre a street demonstration, hunting gazelle by jeep, portrait photography, tobacco, opium, gambling, X-rays, alcohol, binoculars, street light. The story's present is a sort of spectral mid-twentieth century, between the appearance of the first automobiles and the arrival (from the Kennedy Administration onwards) of the Americans.

Behind the story, and just visible through the Prince's bleary eyes and his dusty photographs, are the shadows or phantoms of the two dominant personalities of modern Isfahan: Masud Mirza, the oldest son of

Nassereddin Shah, usually known by the title Zillosultan ('Shadow of the Ruler'), and the powerful and unscrupulous leader of the Isfahan clergy at the end of the nineteenth century, Ayatollah Najafi.

Born in 1850, the son of Shah Nassereddin and the daughter of a Tabrizi housemaid named Iffetosaltaneh ('Chastity of the Monarchy'), Zillosultan was barred from succeeding to the throne by his mother's low birth. Instead, he was appointed to provincial governorships of which the most important, in 1865, was Isfahan. Ambitious, tyrannical and independent, he destroyed some of the city's finest monuments to ensure his father would not wish to move his capital from Tehran. On at least one occasion, in 1879, according to the British Consul of the time, he cornered the city's grain in the hope of making a killing from the starving population.

In the end, Zillosultan became too close to the British for his father's taste. In 1887, he was dismissed from all his posts, but hung on to his life and to Isfahan, where he lingered until the Constitutional Revolution in 1907. In his energy, brutality and passion for hunting, he is the 'Grandfather' and 'the Great Prince' of Golshiri's novel.*

* The only historical figure to appear by name in *The Prince*, as far as I can tell, is Fatimeh Sultan Anisodowleh (d.1897), the senior wife of Nassereddin Shah and the head of his *andarun* (harem).

Zillosultan's rival in the bazaar and on the streets of Isfahan was Sheikh Mohammed Taqi (1846–1914), the great Shia cleric generally known as Aga Najafi after his time at the Shia shrine of Najaf in Iraq, but known in this novel simply as *Aqa* ('His Lordship' or, so as to give a more ecclesiastical feeling, 'His Grace'). In the novel, their rivalry reaches a climax in a scene closely based on a murder that actually occurred.

Zillosultan's son, Akbar Mirza Saremodowleh ('Sword of the Realm') (1885–1975) murdered his mother, Munisosaltaneh ('Companion of the Throne') in June 1907. They had quarrelled over her will. He had accused her of impropriety in her relations with Aqa Nurullah, a younger brother of Aqa Najafi. She took refuge with Nurullah, but he sent her to the house of her married daughter. Akbar Mirza followed her there and shot her three times, one of the bullets penetrating her lung. This exploit did not prevent Saremodowleh from serving as Persian Finance Minister and negotiating in 1919 with Lord Curzon a treaty with Britain so favourable to himself and the British that the Parliament in Tehran never ratified it. Saremodowleh almost saw out the Pahlavis, dying in Paris at a ripe old age in 1975.

One absence in the book is the nation that has so bedevilled the modern history of Iran, the United

Kingdom. Determined to string a row of vassal states along the approaches to their commercial possessions in India, by the mid-nineteenth century the British were well established in southern Iran and intriguing against the profligate Qajars in the north.

The Iranian obsession with British perfidy is the theme of the comic counterpart to *The Prince*, Iraj Pezeshkzad's *Dai Jan Napulion* (*My Uncle Napoleon*) which came out in 1972. We know that Grandfather falls from grace before he can torture Fakhronissa's father to death, but we are not told that it is for accepting the Grand Cross of the Star of India, as Zillosultan in 1887. As it turned out, *The Prince* was published just before thousands of Americans descended on Isfahan to train the Pahlavi air force and weep their hearts out in temporary whisky bars. Like the British, they have left little trace.

'I'd never seen princes even from afar.' In a long interview with the late Kaveh Golestan (who was killed by a landmine while filming for the BBC in Iraqi Kurdistan in 2003), Golshiri said he assembled *Shazdeh Ehtejab* from conversations with a pupil, who had come from a princely background, and from reading. The chief source he mentions is the *Tarikh-e Masud*, Zillosultan's memoir of his travels, hunting exploits and governorships, which was lithographed in the spring of 1907. It is the documentary counterpart of the large volume that the bride Fakhronissa finds amid the chaos of her husband's room:

> Fakhronissa drew her finger across the binding of one of the books. She said: 'Travels in Mazanderan. Lithograph. What trouble I've been to to find a copy of this title! My late father sold everything he had for the puff of smoke that he loved, even his library, but you, oh no . . .'

Golshiri says he read the Tarikh in manuscript in the Municipal Library in Chahar Bagh, the beautiful seventeenth-century promenade in Isfahan. Saremodowleh had donated to that library all the books from the family house, known as the Bagh-e Now or 'New Garden'.*

The other source for the novel, Golshiri said, was the effect produced on him by certain antique objects on public show: Nassereddin Shah's chair, or Reza Khan's

* A new edition of the lithograph, with an index, was printed in Tehran in 1362 (1983 or 1984), and there is a copy of this edition in the British Library.

cane with its tip broken, or the balustrades outside the Bagh e-Now. In addition, though Golshiri does not say this, the Isfahan bazaar was in those days bursting with knick-knacks, sold off by aristocratic families in their precipitous fall down the social scale: tulip vases, old-fashioned revolvers, cast-iron chandeliers, dented armour, European-style furniture, bad Cantonese export porcelain, Kashmir or Kerman shawls, opium pipes decorated with transfers of Nassereddin Shah, and hundreds of stiff portrait photographs (including, I remember, one of a most diffident Master of Wrath, Zillosultan's executioner). In other words, Golshiri did not have to step very far from his house in Forughi Avenue to furnish the Prince's room.

Yet for all Golshiri's sanitary distaste for any contact with Persian nobility, the story does not read like a diatribe, nor a history lesson, nor a pastiche, nor a cuttings job. It does not smell of the lamp. It is perverse that a writer who aspired to the characterless fiction of Robbe-Grillet and claimed to have no affinity to Persian feudalism or the down-at-heel aristocracy that endures to this day in Iran, produced characters of such interest.

Khosrow Ehtejab has not a single redeeming feature. He is not brave, not bright, not kind, not manly, not chivalrous, not rich, not even very wicked. Yet the reader is not indifferent to his fate. Fakhronissa, too, who seems at first just another of the castrating females so beloved of the modernists since Hedayat, is actually something new for Iranian fiction: a black-eyed beauty from a bazaar miniature (cypress-tall, eyelashes like spears, waist like a hair, heart-lassoing tresses etc.), but with a history. Orphaned by opium and marriage politics, nursed on broken sugar, her childhood is narrated with unexpected tenderness. Fakhri has her long moment in front of the mirror (and written, Golshiri said, in a single session). The effect is to enlarge their humanity to the point where the Prince's cruelty to wife and servant is more appalling than his forebear's mass beheadings. A century and a half of Persian history is collapsed into an old man beating up his fat housemaid in a dilapidated provincial town. No writer, as Abbas Milani put it, has so 'captured the pathos of Iran's traditional society'.

The impression conveyed by *The Prince* in both its narrative and its style is not that Iran has no future. More to the point, it has no present. Golshiri writes in a species of past tense in which the auxiliary verb and often the person falls away. Fakhronissa is dead, the Prince is dead and, if Fakhri does survive, it is not into the bright, hard, sensuous reality of Isfahan, city of seminary students and fakers of *papier mâché* pen cases, crows and cement: a city that each day is more ruined and yet seems to have so much more ruin in it. *The Prince* is fiction. It exists merely as an instance of the Iranian knack of making good literature under bad government.

Modern Persian arose in the early Middle Ages as an amalgam of the old speech of Iran and the language of the Arab invaders, and has since taken in a decent sprinkling of Turkish, Russian, French and English. For a stylist such as Golshiri, each language carries mental associations: Persian of the house and homeland, Arabic of the mosque, Turkish of the stable and camp, French of the dressing-table, Russian of the prison, English of the garage. The question, which has bothered translators of Persian since the eighteenth century, is how to reproduce these tones in the key of modern English.

My approach has been as far as possible to use for Persian English words of Anglo-Saxon root, for Arabic Latin and Greek, Turkish for Turkish, Russian for Russian, French for French and English for English. As a language, Persian is quite precise in matters of Court precedence, male costume, the progress of the soul and the rigmarole of keeping the sexes apart, and vague about natural history, female costume, bodily health and what brings the sexes together. In transliterating proper names into English, I have followed no system, but tried to make life easy for the reader who knows no Persian or Arabic.

I would like to thank the author's widow, Farzaneh Taheri, who commissioned this translation of *Shazdeh Ehtejab* into English; Sharan Tabari, Barbara Nestor and Abbas Milani, who encouraged it; and Christopher MacLehose, who edited and published it. Ahmad Golshiri, Mehdi Jami and Andrew Goodson generously helped with Isfahanisms and other difficulties. I would like here to record my gratitude to Dr John Gurney, Lecturer in Persian at Oxford University, who suggested years ago that I study in Isfahan and wrote letters of introduction in his beautiful Persian script.

PRINCE EHTEJAB WAS SUNK IN HIS ARM-chair, his scalding forehead in both hands, coughing away. Once his maid had come upstairs, and once his wife. Fakhri half-opened the door, made to turn on the light, but the Prince stamped his foot. She fled downstairs. Fakhronissa also came in, but the Prince again stamped on the floor.

That evening, as the Prince had turned into the lane, he had seen in the half-light under the trees the wheelchair, Murad lolling as ever in a crumpled heap in it, and Murad's wife peeping with one eye out of her black veil.

'Greetings!'

Murad's wife Hassani said: 'Greetings.'

'You again, Murad? Haven't I told you a hundred times . . .?'

'I know, dear Prince, but there has been no amelioration in my affairs. When I saw there was nothing for dinner, I said: "Hassani, bring out the wheel-chair, perhaps the Prince's generosity will save the day."'

The Prince had put his hand in his pocket and dropped a couple of tumans in Hassani's palm.

Murad said: 'God give you long life and honour, Prince!'

And Hassani, too: 'God bless you, Sir.'

She pushed the wheelchair forward. Drenched in sweat, the Prince went on, the sound of the wheels in his ears till he unlocked his door.

Yet Prince Ehtejab was not at all alarmed. He handed his hat and stick to Fakhri, kissed Fakhronissa on her powdered cheek and went upstairs. He closed the door behind him and sat down in his armchair in the dark. Fakhri herself went into the kitchen, but found she was too disturbed to do anything, and went upstairs. At the sound of the Prince stamping his foot, she fled to her own room, sat in front of the mirror and listened for the smallest sound from the room above to indicate that the Prince was in a better mood, and would stride down the stairs and call:

'Fakhri!'

And Fakhri would stand up, tie on her headscarf and apron, and lay the table. The Prince would wash his hands, dry them and shout:

'Fakhronissa!'

And she'd put the headscarf in the pocket of Fakhri's apron, change her dress, sit down before the mirror, throw on some make-up, comb her hair, then go into the dining-room and sit herself across from the Prince. After dinner, when the Prince had gone upstairs again, then Fakhri would clear the table and wash the dishes, and Fakhronissa would make herself up and go to bed. About midnight, the Prince would come in and whisper:

'Are you asleep, Fakhronissa?'

But this evening, Prince Ehtejab was not himself. He sat as motionless as his own armchair. At times a cough caused his shoulders to shake and he pressed his palms against his hot forehead so he could feel the veins stand out; or drive from his thoughts the gloating looks of Grandfather and Grandmother, Father, Mother, Aunts, even Fakhronissa.

The Prince recognised that, punctual as ever, the family's hereditary fever had struck. But he was not ready to submit to the consumption in the way that the vast room had sweated out and coughed up all its antique objects.

There was a musty smell in the room. Beneath his feet was a rug. The Prince's whole frame occupied just a corner of his ancestral armchair. He could feel the weight and solidity of the chair beneath him. The chirping of the crickets was an endless thread vanishing into the depths of the night.

Perhaps they were in the weedy undergrowth in the garden, or . . . I said: 'Fakhri, pull the curtains to! I don't want to see any of that damn street light!' Fakhri said: 'Prince dear, won't you let me open the window for a nice bit of fresh air?'

'Shut up, you! Just do as I say.'

Fakhri had her apron on. She had a broom in her hand. Her headscarf with the flower pattern. Dark and lively eyes. Open mouth. A row of coarse, white teeth.

'At least let me dust the photograph frames.'

'There's no need. Don't you see? Your job is to see to the other rooms.'

Fakhronissa had such a little mouth! So little that when she laughed, she showed only a couple of white teeth. She used to look down at him through the thick glass of her spectacles. The contours of her neck fell sharp and straight to her shoulders and arms, covered (or not) by her dress of white lace. She said: 'Prince, what a mess in here! You should tidy up a bit. Or have the servants . . .' She drew a long white finger down the horse's mane. The horse was white with chestnut splashes. The line she made ran the length of the mane to the tail.

Fakhronissa was standing beside a coach and four. She was wearing her white lace dress, pleated at the breast. He couldn't tell if those eyes behind the thick glass were looking at him or not. What she said was:

'Fakhri, do you have matches?'

Fakhri dug into the pocket of her apron and said: 'Please.'

'You light them,' said Fakhronissa.

She pointed at the chandeliers with a hand that came, no doubt, from a pleated sleeve. Fakhri lit the chandeliers. She lit every single candle. How bright it was! As for Fakhronissa, she surely did not blink. She said: 'Light the candelabra as well.' She gestured with that hand that . . . or she did no such thing. I said: 'What's this all about, Fakhronissa?' She said: 'Nothing the matter, is there, Prince?' One couldn't see her eyes. One never saw them properly. The flames flickered in the glass of her spectacles. The book she had under her arm she placed on the mantelpiece. She lifted the hem of her skirt, made her way through the clutter, and picked up Great-grandfather's clock and wound it. It began to tick. Then Grandfather's clock and Father's and even the pocket-watches, she wound them all. She said: 'Don't just stand there, Fakhri. Come and help.' Fakhri helped her. I helped her, too. Grandfather's clock chimed, loud and clear. Toy footmen popped out, five of them, tall, with curled moustachios. They put their hands to their chests, bowed and disappeared. Fakhronissa said: 'Did you observe that, dear Prince? That could only have been a present from the Russian *chargé d'affaires* to His Radiant and Hallowed Majesty.' With her finger she was rubbing the dust from the lower rim of the clock. I said: 'Fakhronissa, it's driving me mad.' So many hands moving on so many faces, and ticking away against one another. Little soldiers appeared, carrying carbines. Fakhronissa burst out laughing. She came to attention and saluted. Her spectacles slipped down her nose. She went on laughing. Her eyes were damp with tears, I'm sure. She doubled up and slapped her thighs. Her two plaits lay on her chest. She had a round bosom. She laughed and laughed. Her laughter soared above the ticking clocks. Fakhri, too, was laughing. Or rather, her fat lips quivered.

Fakhronissa frowned. She was holding one of the golden wine-cups. She leaned forward and brandished it in the Prince's face:

'Look, Prince.'

The Prince looked at it. On the beaker was a naked woman, hair flying. She held an apple in her hand. A vine with two leaves covered her breasts. Her stomach and thighs were thick with dust. Fakhronissa said:

'Fakhri dear, put two of these on the table.'

The Prince said: 'Really! These are . . .'

'I would like to know how the wine tastes from them.'

Now she had a revolver in her hand. She asked: 'It's loaded?'

'I don't know,' said the Prince.

Fakhronissa said: 'Let's see. Give it to me, girl!'

She put her hand in Fakhri's apron and pulled out a duster. She began with the barrel and was just . . . The Prince cried: 'Don't touch the trigger.'

She said: 'Were you frightened, Prince?'

She frowned. Her spectacles still rested on the tip of her nose. With the barrel pointed at the wall, she cleaned it and then put on the safety catch. Then she took up the shotguns and cartridge-belts, cleaning them one by one, and dusted the red deer's antlers. She took off her spectacles. Fakhri was standing behind her mistress, her hands in the pockets of her apron. Fakhronissa turned about and looked at the Prince:

'He was seventeen years old. One of Great-grandfather's trophies, no doubt.' Then with a loud and manly voice: '"Up to that point we had never taken such a stag. We were quite pleased with the result. The tenantry contributed three Kashmir shawls, two bay horses and three hundred tumans in money."'

She burst out laughing. With her finger she flicked a crystal beaker. The fragile crystal rang amid the ticking clocks. It was like a sip of water, cold water. She flicked it again. This time, the ring was louder. The clock hands crept round, slow and assured, crawling towards the hours when footmen, soldiers or dancing-girls would pop out. Gradually, the ticking swallowed the brittle shiver of the glass. And Fakhronissa once more flicked the glass with her long, white finger. The ring of the glass trilled amid all those sounds, took off, swelled and spread and vanquished them all. Then there was just the ringing of the glass, which fell away and lost itself amid the insistent and permanent cacophony of the clocks. There were short swords and helmets on the table. And pen-cases of mother-of-pearl. She picked up Great-grandfather's helmet. 'Come, Prince, let's try it on.' I said: 'Please leave it alone. Not two days a bride and you're at it again?' She put the helmet on my head. It almost covered my eyes. Fakhronissa bent and peered up at me through her spectacles. 'It doesn't suit you one little bit, Prince. Surely, Qamarodowleh* and the gardener didn't . . . eh? Truly, not a grain of your forefathers' Magnificence has come down to you.'

* 'Moon of the Realm.' Presumably that was the title given to the Prince's mother.

'Have you quite finished, Fakhronissa?'

She lifted off the helmet and put it on the table. The shelves were stuffed with bits and pieces. She flicked at them with the rag. A cloud of dust rose up and she stepped back. 'I presume the manservants and housemaids have all perished.' I said: 'I gave the order that nobody . . .' I kept the key by me. She put a finger under my chin and lifted my head. Her finger was cold, just like her body, so cold and white, and elongated and bloodless. Her breasts were small and round, her hair soft. She'd said: 'I like the dark, Prince. Remember to put that lamp out before you come to bed.' I looked at her: she was staring straight at me, her finger under my chin. 'Gave the order, did you? So there is some of the old ancestral blood in you after all.' I said: 'For heaven's sake, not in front of Fakhri . . .' She burst out laughing. 'You're scared of Fakhri? She's a quiet girl, Prince.' She stroked Fakhri's hair. Fakhri shuddered, looked down at the carpet, no doubt, and its flower-pattern. Fakhronissa said: 'Fakhri, my love, when you have dusted up here tomorrow, I'll show you how everything should be. This drawing-room is really too poky. The books at least you can bring to my room.' I had stacked the books against the wall. Fakhronissa drew her finger across the binding of one of the books. She said: '*Travels in Mazanderan.*

Lithographed. What trouble I've been to to find a copy of this title. My late father sold everything he had for the puff of smoke that he loved, even his library, but you, oh no . . .' With her finger, she pushed back my hair, which had, no doubt, flopped down over my forehead, and said: 'If you do not mind, I wish to purloin your books.'

Fakhri, who was still there beside her mistress, said: 'The candles are smoking, Ma'am.'

'Well, blow them out. Every one of them.'

Fakhri put the candles out, one by one. Fakhronissa said:

'Fakhri dear, turn on the electric light. But stay right where you are. And careful with the vases, girl.'

Fakhronissa's cold fingers passed over the Prince's ears, his cheeks, his chin, and then his mouth. The Prince kissed the fingers. They moved on to his nose and his eyes. His eyelids were closed. Light hands were on the Prince's shoulders. The Prince stretched out a hand and took a tress of Fakhronissa's hair and very gently drew his hand down it to the tip. The hair was long and the Prince had to stretch. Something cold and heavy rested in his hand. Fakhronissa laughed and said:

'You're such a slowcoach, Prince. When are you going to get moving, eh?'

It was Grandfather's revolver. It was heavy and cold.

The room teemed with the endless ticking of the clocks, the musty smell, half-burned candles, and perfume wafting over from Fakhronissa standing in the gloom. The Prince cried out:

'I should have opened the window so that at least the musty smell . . .'

He began to cough. He knew that however hard he coughed he could never shake the big door-panes and window-panes. And still he coughed.

Prince Ehtejab knew that there was no point . . . that he couldn't . . . that Grandfather would always be there, as in the black-and-white photograph, or like a skin stuffed with straw: a faint presence that would linger on in all these books and pictures and contradictory stories. He would have liked to have known, if only for his own or Fakhronissa's sake, would have liked to understand what it was that inside that skin, beyond the light and dark of the photographs or between the lines of all those books . . . He shouted:

'I have to do something!'

And he burst out coughing. And in the midst of all the valets, chief eunuchs, footmen; amid the shouts of, 'Eyes away! Out of the way!'; and the women and slave-girls splashing and tussling in the pool . . . Were they naked? Great-grandfather would certainly have been laughing.

And enchanted with the scene . . . would have tossed gold coins among them while the women and the slave-girls scrambled after them, a mass of living, white flesh, heaving, giggling, coalescing, with here and there a hand or foot poking out. And when the heap of flesh disintegrated, Great-grandfather would have scattered more gold coins. Over there, beyond all this, Grandfather would be standing. Or perhaps be seated? An indistinct impression of a short and plump child, or maybe of a tall and thin with thick hair, or maybe . . . and eyes of . . .? With sword and cap and boots and gleaming buttons. And tutors, the Minister, counsellors. The Governor of . . . who knows where. And should the opportunity have arisen, when there was nobody to receive ceremoniously, and no clergy were coming to pray for His Highness, and no Generals to kiss his hallowed feet . . .

'If you put out a sparrow's eyes, how far can it fly?'

And he coughed, loud and long. He knew that he could not continue and left Grandfather as he was, seated on his throne or astride a well-schooled horse or beyond that formless, living, giggling mound of flesh.

Grandfather stroked his thick moustache, coughed and shook in the picture frame. Once the dust had settled, the Prince could make out Grandfather's sallow face, the deep furrows in his forehead and the two fleshy jowls of his double chin. Grandfather shook the dust off his sleeve. His ceremonial tunic was bleached. A flaw in the photographic plate was still visible on Grandfather's left shoulder. The bleached and shadowy contours of Grandfather's hands seemed to be on the point of taking shape. But it did not occur to the Prince to rise to his feet, as in the old days, and with his hand to his chest, saying over and over:

'Yes, Sire!'

From jowls of flesh beneath thick, greying eyebrows black pupils stared out at the Prince and the walls and the stove. The hand which was now a lump of flesh and nerves reached out and took the silver-topped cane from off the shelf. The pommel he wiped with his handkerchief. The contours of his lips were as pale as ever. Grandfather's chair stood on a dais. The Jew straightened his spectacles, rolled his tongue in his mouth, shuffled across the floor and squinted short-sightedly at Grandfather's chair. But when the Prince saw Grandfather advance on the chair shaking his stick, he wanted to cry out: 'Rascal of a Jew! And in the presence of Grandfather!' And throw him out of the room. The Jew stroked his thin beard:

'My dear Prince, this chair is all worn out. I swear by God, I'll never shift it.'

The Prince said: 'You shameless villain, if Grand-father finds out . . .'

'Well, if one of those *nouveaux riches* turns up, then well and good.'

Prince Ehtejab knew that that rascal of a Jew could not grasp that it was hard for him, that one simply could dispose of fifteen years of memories for a pittance. But now that Grandfather had sat back down again in the chair of his ancestors and the main drawing-room taken shape again with its dais and windows of stained-glass and doors and the stucco-work flower motifs on the walls and even the two alcoves and the mirror-work on the wall pillars; and the shelves were lined with their old dishes and ewers, and the chandeliers lit and a nice fire burning in the stove and that familiar smell of burning wood, then he could say to Grandfather:

'Please be assured, Your Highness' chair was worth more to me than this money, this . . .'

And Grandfather bellowed:

'Couldn't you have spared just this one thing?'

And he raised his silver-topped cane and made as if to bring it down once again on his grandson's ankles. He held back and said:

'The fact is I did sell a great deal of land to pay off your father's debaucheries, but you, you're not worth spit. You sold me for a miserable ten thousand tumans!'

The Prince wanted to say: 'As I suggested to you, I merely . . . ' But when Grandfather was simply unable to grasp that it wasn't possible any more to mount the carriage and trot down the city boulevards and that the horses must eat, and the stable-lad and the coachman, and that old fellow must not only with his own hand groom the horses but take bread from the mouths of his wife and children to have something to feed the beasts, and early each morning wash down the rickety old carriage . . .

'At your service, Your Excellency Prince Ehtejab.'

The coachman had his old cap in one hand, the other at his breast, and bowed deeply. He pointed with his cap at the carriage. Steam rose up all around it. The Prince was astonished to see that the two points of Murad Khan's moustache, which had hung down for years on each side of his mouth, now bristled in points at his cheeks.

"Tya service, Prince.'

The Prince climbed up and threw himself on the banquette. Murad Khan put his cap back on and sat down on the box in front. With a Hee! Hee!, he whipped up the horses and set off at the gallop down the gravel drive through the garden.

'Murad Khan! Slow down!'

'Don't be afraid, dear Prince.'

The carriage was passing through the streets. The people were turning and staring. The Prince saw how the fog of the horses' breath mingled with that of Murad Khan and how the coachman straightened his bent back and whipped on the horses. The horses' hooves rang on the asphalt.

'Hisssh!'

At a crossroads, Murad Khan reined in the horses and the Prince saw him bend double and then fall. The horses' hooves must have skidded on the icy asphalt. He was lying right between the horses' feet and the wheels of the carriage. The carriage was still dragging over the ground. He didn't let out a cry, merely said:

'Don't worry about me, Prince. I can manage.'

Prince Ehtejab truly wanted to explain to Grandfather why he had booted out the servants, with punches and kicks, even Murad, and said:

'I was sick and tired of the tap-tap-tap of his bloody crutches.'

Grandfather shouted:

'You threw him out, you son of a bitch, so he could go about and tell everybody all the dreadful things that I, the Great Prince, had done. How I did to death with my own hand my slut of a mother, that I went to the house of the Seal of Islam, that Refuge of Faithful Men and Pious Women, and said to His Grace's servants: "Tell her to come outside." How the servants went in and came out and said to me, the Great Prince: "His Grace has given instructions that any person who seeks asylum in the shadow of His Grace's patronage . . ." How I struck them across the chest and strode into the women's quarters.*

'The women were seated round the basin. They shrieked and ran indoors. My slut of a mother ran to her room, barred the door and threw her weight against it. But before the servants could come with their 'His Grace wishes . . .' I smashed one of the coloured panes and with a couple of shots gave her her quietus so she should not again make the error of seeking the protection of His Grace's patronage . . .'

The Prince wanted to ask, 'But why, Grandfather, did she seek asylum in His Grace's household?' but already Grandfather was marching up and down the room, twirling his silver-topped cane about him. He cried out:

* Large Persian households of this period were divided into the *biruni*, the 'outside' or public rooms, and the *andarun*, the 'inside' or private rooms where the women and children lived and male strangers were not admitted.

'And you, why did you throw Murad out with his broken legs, so he would go about saying . . .?'

'I had them make him a wheelchair. And when his wife died, I found him another woman for his old age, so he'd stay quietly at home. But was that the end of it? Even in the morning he'd be coming down the avenue in the middle of the garden. Then Hassani, his wife, would help him up all those stairs. And when I heard the creak of the wheels I knew he was back again to tell me: "Dear Prince, Ghulamreza Khan has gone to his reward."'

Grandfather asked: 'Ghulamreza Khan?'

'Don't you recall him?' said the Prince. 'The son of Hajji Samsam, the grandson of Fakhrozaman, and a full cousin of yours, a prince of the blood,* who appeared only at official receptions and was always fiddling with his watch-chain. He did not dare smoke in front of you, in the presence of the Great Prince.'

'Ah!'

'He caught gangrene. His whole body swelled up and his face was so puffed up that you could not recognise him. God have mercy on him. He died in terrible pain. He was bedridden a whole year.'

Grandfather swished his cane through the air. 'So it

* That is, his mother was of aristocratic stock. The fate of a son of a morganatic marriage is told in the next pages.

was for this kind of chatter you threw him out of the house, eh?'

'No, it wasn't just that. After he had announced the deaths of all my cousins, male and female, both full- and half-blood on my father's side, and my cousins, male and female, both full- and half-blood on my mother's side, I said to myself: "Peace and quiet, at last." Yet the very next day, he turned up again and before the call to midday prayer. I said: "Murad Khan, how are you?"'

Murad Khan chewed on his moustache and ran his hand over his hair. 'God's mercy on you, dear Prince . . .'

Hassani leaned against a pillar. Only one of her eyes was visible.

'Well?' said the Prince.

Murad rubbed his hands down his legs and rolled himself a cigarette. 'Dear Prince, did you hear that Hajji Taqi had passed over?'

Prince Ehtejab looked down at his own hands. They were small and white.

'Hajji Taqi?'

'He was a grocer. He had a shop in the little covered bazaar. He was a God-fearing man, Prince. He never missed the evening prayer. Last night, he passed away on his own prayer-rug. What a peaceful way to go!' And the Prince said: 'Do you see what I mean, Grandfather? Even if nobody had died, he'd still come down that avenue, and up those stairs, and roll himself a cigarette and pour out his heart:

'I was a member of his mounted detachment. We saddled up the horses and slung our rifles in our shoulder-belts. We were issued with a couple of cartridge-belts. The Great Prince had said: "Make sure you don't kill any of the tenants!" We galloped to the village of Charnuyeh. We posted a couple of cavalrymen at the ford so that Great-uncle shouldn't escape. Once we had established that there was no resistance, we went into the village. There, too, there was no sign of any armed men. The tenants stood gaping by their house doors. The Great Prince bellowed: "Get lost, you lot!" They all ran inside and bolted their doors. We galloped to the manor house. Great-uncle came out to receive us. His hands were shaking. He was holding some papers and was saying over and over: "Exalted brother, here are the title deeds. I want nothing for myself. Just please consent to allow me to stay in the village with my wife and children."

'The Great Prince chewed the end of his moustache. He dismounted from his horse and handed the reins to me. The cavalrymen dragged Great-uncle inside. They fetched his children and his wife, who was from the village. The Great Prince said:

' "How many brats have you?" '

'I did not say that,' said Grandfather. 'I knew the answer. What I said was: "In no time at all you've made three children, you useless peasant."'

The Prince said: 'Great-uncle still had the title deeds in his hands. The children must have been clutching their mother's skirts. One of the cavalrymen had the wife by the arms. And you, you lashed out, struck Great-uncle in the face with the back of your hand, laid him out on the floor with a single blow. The title deeds flew everywhere. One of the cavalrymen tied Great-uncle's hands and feet. And you picked up a cushion, set it on his face, and sat on it. Or so Murad said.'

Grandfather said: 'He had sent me a message, saying, "This estate is also my paternal inheritance. You and I, we have the same rights." He, the son of some village scrubber without two pence to rub together, and I the Great Prince!'

The Prince said: 'What happened, Murad said, was that His Royal Highness had been hunting near the village of Charnuyeh, and had married the girl on a temporary contract.* After some time, she sent word

* Iranian Islam disapproves of sex outside marriage, and has devised even for casual encounters the institution of *sigheh*, 'temporary marriage', which gives some rights to the woman.

that she was pregnant and His Royal Highness made the child the present of a couple of villages.'

Grandfather said: 'The marriage contract was for just one month only.'

The Prince went on: 'According to Murad, the Great Prince sat down on the cushion and said: "Cigarette!" Up to that day I'd never seen the Great Prince put a cigarette to his lips. I lost my nerve. My hands were trembling. The cavalrymen stood in a circle against the walls. Great-uncle's wife stood with her mouth agape, but she wasn't weeping. Great-uncle was still groaning as I rolled the cigarette and handed it to the Great Prince. Your Great-uncle struggled. I lit the cigarette. The Great Prince sat there on the cushion, drew on his cigarette and blew the smoke through his nostrils. Great-uncle was still tossing and turning. I saw his feet moving.'

I asked him: 'What about his hands? Had they turned scarlet?'

He said: 'I didn't see.'

'But they had bound him fast?'

'Assuredly!'

'And what about the children?'

'There were two girls and a boy. They had dark eyes, Prince.'

'I know that. But what did the children do?'

'I don't know. I didn't see.'

'And what about Grandfather?'

'I told you. The whole time I didn't take my eyes off the Great Prince, sitting there on the cushion and smoking his cigarette.'

'What about Great-uncle's wife?'

'I have an idea that she wept. Then she was suddenly quiet. Maybe one of the cavalrymen shut her up.'

'Did they shut the children up, too?'

'Possibly.'

'What about Grandfather?'

'He was seated on the cushion. When he finished his cigarette, he stubbed out the butt on Great-uncle's hand, stood up and said: "Toss them in the well." We threw Great-uncle in first.'

'How old was he?'

'I imagine he was twenty-two years old.'

'And then?'

'Then we threw his wife in. The children we also chucked into the well and piled rocks on top of them.'

'Then what happened?'

'Nothing at all. As we were leaving the manor, the Great Prince shot one of the tenantry. Well, he had come into the manor.'

Then Prince Ehtejab saw his grandfather seated on

that jewelled and inlaid throne, blowing smoke through his nostrils and tipping his ash into an inlaid ashtray. Then he let the image go and Grandfather slipped back behind his court uniform, as in the photograph. And he coughed.

Grandmother gathered up the folds of her long white wedding dress so that it would not pick up dust from the picture frame. As she stepped out and saw her little angel took no notice of her, she smoothed out the creases in her dress and cast a glance at Grandfather. Grandfather was still smoking his cigarette. And Grandmother, though she was still young and slender, let out a couple of small, dry coughs as in her old age. And Prince Ehtejab just sat there, would not stand up and ask: 'Would you permit me, Grandmother, to summon Dr Abu Nuvas?'

Now Father, who was still galloping round on his bay horse, saw that Khosrow had not even risen to kiss his grandmother's hand, reined in his horse and jumped down. Was Murad there as well? And Father slapped his whip against the leg of his riding-boot. The buttons gleamed on his riding-jacket. Prince Ehtejab was still seated. His burning forehead rested on his hands. The horse turned, looked about, pawed the ground, whinnied and rose on its hind legs. Its mane filled the picture frame. It broke into a trot and disappeared behind the little hills in the picture. A ribbon of dust hung in the air over the line of hills.

Father's face was drained of colour. His cap was in his hands. His hair hung in bangs over his forehead. His clothes were soaked through. Had it really rained so hard? His epaulettes hung down from his shoulders. He had come just at sundown. Grandfather made a signal and Grandmother and the aunts, who were in a circle around him, left the room. The older aunt had Grandfather by the shoulders.

Grandfather said: 'Alright. Out with it.'

Father swept the hair off his forehead, shifted his cap from hand to hand, tore the epaulettes off his shoulders and put them in his pocket.

'It's all over. I have tendered my resignation.'

Grandfather gripped the handle of his cane, swung it through the air and pressed the point against Father's chest.

'Well then, you'll have to leave this Godforsaken country for a year or two until enough water has passed under the bridge.'

Father looked down at Prince Ehtejab who was now standing by him. He took Khosrow by the hand. Father's hand was cold.

'Why should I? I was following orders.'

'Following orders, were you? Then why have you allowed the responsibility to fall on you?'

'I had orders not to permit anybody to pass down that boulevard.'

Grandfather coughed. Older Aunt appeared. Khosrow could see only her head. Her eyes were completely white. Grandfather said:

'And so?'

'Suddenly, they appeared. There must have been several thousand of them. I could see just the dark outlines of their heads and their open mouths. One or two of them had clubs in their hands. I lost my nerve.'

Again Grandfather coughed. The point of his cane was now on the ground and he leaned on it. He was quite pale. He was chewing on the end of his moustaches. Father's hand was in Khosrow's hair.

'I never wanted it to be like that. It never occurred to me that that could happen to people, that they could be so easily flattened. As they set off they were like a wave. Hands, clubs and gaping mouths. I gave the order: "Open fire with the machine guns!" There was a whirr and a grinding and a hail and the wave of men retreated. The dark heads passed into the distance.'

'And that's it?' said Grandfather.

Father said: 'I didn't look behind me. However, I think that behind us there were just amputated hands lying there, maybe still grasping a club or mace or two.'

Grandfather coughed again. 'So, now you feel bad about it?'

He was looking at Khosrow. Prince Ehtejab glued himself to his father's leg. His father's hand was still twined in Khosrow's hair. Grandfather said: 'Or are you just scared they'll toss you into prison?'

The cough interrupted him. The aunts appeared, even Grandmother. Grandfather was still coughing. And now Father was pacing up and down the room. He had his cap in his hand, trailing his riding-crop along the floor.

Father existed behind that uniform of his and the smoke-rings he used to blow from his mouth and the dark mascaraed eyes of the women or the trees. The trees shaded the entire width of the gravel avenue. Further away, it was even shadier. The branches and leaves made a sort of barrel-vault over the avenue, a green barrel-vault. Prince Ehtejab, who felt cold, watched his father kick up the gravel with the toe of his boot and pace towards the green vault. Khosrow was seated on the kerb beside the avenue. He had to turn his head round so far to keep his father in view that his neck ached. He still had the red-and-white ball in his hand. As Father came up and passed him, with those long and measured strides, he would toss the ball into the water-channel; then bend down and, all the while counting his father's steps, follow the ball with his hand and look up to watch one of the aunts, in the long, black dress she always wore, come back to the window to watch Father.

The tiles in the channel were green and white. At the sound of the gate, Father turned into the trees along the avenue. The servants went to the gate and came back this time with a paper. Grandfather, doubtless, would have taken the paper, glanced at it and burst out: 'Sons of bitches! As if I hid treasure under the bed!'*

The sound of Grandfather's coughing could be heard through the windows. He was in the middle saloon. Older Aunt picked up the skirt of her black dress and came down the stairs.

'Khosrow, where is your papa?'

Prince Ehtejab pointed to the bosky line of trees on the far side of the avenue. Aunt had run down the steps and along the avenue to the Prince, then turned off into

* Reza Shah, who took power in 1921, was ruthless in confiscating the property of the Qajar aristocracy in the later 1920s and the 1930s.

the trees. And Khosrow no longer needed to throw his ball into the canal.

Prince Ehtejab knew that it was now the turn of the aunts. And duly the aunts came forward with their long black dresses and white eyes and sat down. The Prince resisted. He knew that beyond the black-and-white of the photograph of the aunts much was concealed. If he tried, he might find something in the darkness further over there, something valuable maybe, that might help him make Fakhronissa anew, or even himself. But now that he had scratched out their eyes with his pen-knife, and the aunts were so far away, their skin draped in those long, black dresses . . . He had let that be a long time ago. Once again the two dark walls closed on the Prince with their whispers.

'Khosrow Khan!'

'Khosrow! Come here!'

Older Aunt said: 'Khosrow Khan, it is beneath the dignity of a prince to take the kite away from the gardener's son.'

But Khosrow wanted to fly the kite. The two walls had risen each side of him with their eyes eaten by termites. And Khosrow could only think about how he could get away. The wind was getting up. The kite with its red-and-green wings and tail floated in the blue sky. It stopped fluttering. The line raced through Khosrow's small hands and the kite climbed higher. Only the body of the kite was visible. The delicate ribbons on the corners and tail were about to vanish in the blue sky. The gardener's son stood by, shading his eyes with his hand. As the wind freshened, the pale, soft hands of the Prince were not strong enough to hold the line. The Prince wanted the gardener's son to come and help him bring the kite to earth. But there was Older Aunt, crying out:

'Khosrow Khan, you should be ashamed of yourself!'

The line slipped out of the Prince's hands. The kite grew smaller and smaller. The tail and red-and-green wings vanished into the blue heaven. The gardener's son ran off and disappeared in the trees. And Prince Ehtejab still had his head in his hands. His hands were shaking, but he had stopped coughing.

It was Grandfather who started. He burst out into a long, dry cough. His shoulders shook from the force of his coughing and the Prince heard the stained-glass windows in the audience hall rattle. And he who was so small and thin stood beside Grandfather's jewel-studded throne. He held his father's hand. Father was wearing his jewelled court robes. He carried a sword in his belt. Beside Father the others had formed up in order of precedence: non-uterine paternal cousins etc. . . . and on the other side of the room sat the clergy with their round beards and black or white turbans, hands before their stomachs, telling their prayer-beads. Then came a line of footmen with their handlebar moustaches and black baize caps. They leaned on silver-handled maces and stared straight ahead. The Prince turned and looked his father in the face. He could see only the turned-up points and black mass of his moustaches.

From the door opposite a tall chamberlain came in, carrying a tray covered in a Kashmir shawl. He walked round the fountain. Were there fish in the fountain? The jets of water rose high into the air. When he came before Grandfather, he bowed low. Grandfather pulled back the Kashmir shawl. The tray was piled with silver and gold coins and purses tied at the mouth with thread. Grandfather picked up one of the purses. One of the uterine paternal cousins stepped forward. He kissed Grandfather's hand. Grandfather handed him the purse and began to cough, a long fit of dry coughing. All the coloured panes in the windows of the audience hall rattled. The clergy had their prayer-beads in their laps. The footmen turned about to see what was happening. The chamberlain stood there with his tray in front of Grandfather. A new fit of coughing took hold. Grand-father took out his white handkerchief and pressed it to his mouth. As he bent double, shoulders shaking, the stained glass rattled for a second time. Father let go of Prince Ehtejab's hand. Once again the Prince saw the prayer-beads. As the long-drawn-out dry coughing again rose up, the Prince heard the chandeliers ring and saw the files of people begin to disperse. He could no longer see Grandfather. But he could hear him coughing and could see the thicket of people reflected in the pier-glasses into infinity.

He sat with his sunken cheeks among the women. Mother had on her black lace headscarf, knotted at the throat. The termites had eaten out the eyes of the women on each side and above Mother's head. Mother stood up among the women. The hand that up to now had been hidden behind one of the women she stretched out in the hope that Prince Ehtejab would get up and take it. But the Prince went on sitting with his head bowed. Mother's hand was white. Her hands were small with greenish veins. And the Prince knew that Mother was now looking over the women in the photograph one by one. Mother picked up the skirts of her long black dress and came and stood right in front of Grandfather, curtseyed and kissed first Grandfather's hand and then Grandmother's.

Grandfather's cough was becoming drier and softer.

The aunts went noiselessly to and fro. Dr Abu Nuvas appeared under the vault of trees in his long gown, smelling of his infusions. His paternal cousin, Fakhronissa, was still seated within her photograph. She had a carnation in the corner of her mouth and a large, leather-bound volume on her lap. Her long white fingers rested on the binding, while, in her right hand, she held her prescription spectacles.

Fakhronissa cleaned her spectacles with a white handkerchief and put them on. She stood up. She gathered up her white lace dress, stepped over the book which had fallen onto the arabesques of the carpet, and came down from out of the photograph. The carnation she had in her mouth she put in a flower vase and used those delicate, white fingers to flick the dust from her hair. And Prince Ehtejab, who was well aware how clumsy Fakhri was and how she never remembered to let two bangs of hair fall on her forehead, cried out:

'Don't smear so much lipstick on those fat lips of yours! Can't you get it into your head that you must make yourself up like Fakhronissa? And that damned beauty spot should be at the left corner of your mouth, not on your peasant's gob!'

Fakhri burst into tears and buried her face, stinging from the Prince's slaps, in her hands. Her fat, fleshy shoulders had been squeezed into one of her mistress's hand-me-down dresses.

'But, Prince, she was a lady, a real lady. And what am I supposed to do with my hands? Fakhronissa's fingers were so white and slender.'

The Prince wiped away Fakhri's tears. He took up her fat, fleshy hands, that reeked of soap and straw-and-mud* in his own that were pale and bloodless.

'Don't be upset, I like these hands, these hands as they are. Your job is to try and do your face like Fakhronissa. Let your hair fall onto your bosom. And let's have a few of these on your forehead. And in the evening put on the white lace dress with the scalloped collar.'

Fakhri grasped the Prince's hands. She put her lips to his burning hot skin. She knelt before him.

'And the dishes? Who is going to wash the dishes? And the rooms? Who's going to sweep the rooms?'

The Prince ran his hand through Fakhri's hair. Then with his thumb he wiped away the tears that had made a furrow down her make-up.

'That's for Fakhri to worry about. You are the mistress of this household, is that clear? It's for Fakhri to wash the dishes and sweep the rooms. And when I pinch

* Before modern soap became widespread in Iran, a mixture of straw and mud was used to clean dishes.

52

her bottom she's to cackle and run off to the kitchen.'

Fakhronissa put the finishing touches to her make-up. The carnation was still in the vase.

The aunts with their long black dresses and eyes eaten by termites stood beside the Great Prince. Grandfather was sunk in his armchair. Father approached and stood before the Great Prince, looked first at the aunts, then the carpet rosettes, and said:

'Please permit me to absent myself.'

'Where?'

Grandfather coughed.

Father said: 'I am sick and tired of wearing myself out with the tenantry. I can't go on.'

The aunts took hold of Grandfather's shoulders, as he spoke:

'Sick and tired, are you? Can't go on running your own estates, can you? All these villages and tenants getting to you, are they? Feel like entering somebody else's service, do you? Well, do as you like. Go, if you like. But know that you are no longer my son.'

And the aunts chimed in: 'We think it's a shame that you, the Prince's only hope, should act as these people's* servant.'

* Presumably, the Pahlavis, as Reza Khan called his family.

And Younger Aunt said: 'Brother, don't do it, least of all now . . .'

And she indicated Grandfather. Father made fists of his hands. When he saw that Khosrow was standing right beside him, he stroked the soft hair of Prince Ehtejab.

'Look, Father dear, land doesn't pay any more, as you yourself are aware . . .'

Grandfather reached for his stick, which Older Aunt was holding. Younger Aunt said:

'So for money and a bit more income you're willing to enter these people's service?'

She began to cry. She laid her head on the shoulder of Older Aunt. Grandfather burst out coughing. Dr Abu Nuvas stood above him. As the coughing fit passed, Grandfather pushed the doctor aside and said:

'So, land doesn't pay any more? That time I gave you a village to save your useless skin, it paid well enough. When I paid for all your debaucheries, it paid alright. But now I am about to leave the world, and you have to take responsibility and be the pillar of the family, it doesn't pay any more, eh?'

'Permit me, dear Father, it is not my intention . . .'

And Grandfather cried out:

'Oh, go to hell! No son of mine, no son of the Great

Prince, is going to work for these parvenus and carry their medal on his chest. I spit on you.'

Prince Ehtejab knew that now his mother was crying. He saw his mother stand up and go and sit back down in the picture frame and wipe away her tears. The background of the photograph was bleached white. Grandfather coughed again and the coloured goblets rattled. Grandmother was not coughing. The reek of infusions filled the room and the hall and hung over the gravel walk. Grandmother said:

'Dear Prince, your son is grown up. He knows what he is doing.'

Older Aunt said: 'Forugh Sultan, it would be better if you . . .'

'. . . kept your thoughts to yourself,' said Younger Aunt.

Grandmother burst out coughing. She put her handkerchief to her mouth. Her shoulders shook, but she still managed to blurt out:

'Prince, I have only one son left to me, and now you allow these witches . . .'

Older Aunt said: 'Witch! So I'm a witch, am I?'

Younger Aunt burst into tears and put her head on Older Aunt's shoulder.

The Great Prince said: 'Keep quiet, you!' And he

gripped the arm of his chair. Everybody fell silent. Inside the photograph frame, Mother was crying.

The horse came out from among the hills. Its saddle and harness glittered in the sunshine. It whinnied. Khosrow turned round and gazed at it. Prince Ehtejab had his head down, but he could see the horse come up on its hind legs. Its mane blocked out the hills in the photograph. The tassels on its head-band had fallen over its eyes. Murad's moustache tips reached to his ears and his shadow fell on the window-panes and the carpet. Father said:

'Murad Khan, have you saddled the horse?'

Khosrow, too, began to cry. Prince Ehtejab watched as the aunts ran after Father's horse as far as the vault of branches and leaves.

Four roan horses with black harness pulled the coach. The manes and tails of the horses were black. The velvet covering of the coach was also black. Without doubt, Murad Khan had taken hold of the bridle of one of the lead horses and was walking on. Prince Ehtejab and Grandmother and Father were seated on the banquettes of the coach. In the mirrors Father's frowning face could be seen. The velvet inside was red. The gold-braided frills of the velvet were soft. It was Grandfather's coach. The black bier ahead shook and bobbed above the heads of the crowd. Murad Khan was wearing a ceremonial tunic and a black sash diagonally across his back. Outrunners, also with black sashes, drove the people back. Father's gloves were black. Horsemen trotted on each side of the coach. The Prince said:

'I want to get down.'

Grandmother said: 'You'll be trampled by the horses.'

The Prince said: 'I don't care. I want to get down.'

Father took Khosrow firmly by the hand. He frowned. The buttons of his tunic gleamed. The entire route had been sprinkled with water. The people stood on both sides. Women had their children by the hand. There were people even in the trees and on the roofs. The horsemen rode on. They had laid Grandfather on the bier and spread a length of Kashmir shawl over him. He coughed no more. His moustaches hung down and the wrinkles on his face had been smoothed away. His forehead gleamed. Only Mother and the aunts were weeping. Younger Aunt had put her head on the shoulder of Older Aunt. Horsemen rode up and down. The aunts were in the coach behind. Mother sat in the next coach back. On both sides of the street, behind the gutter and the trees, people were standing. Grandmother was not there, only Father and Mother. The aunts were in the coach behind.

Murad, dressed in black velvet coat, black trousers and black kid gloves, gleaming boots and Astrakhan hat, was leading a horse by the bridle. Ahead of him, a crowd marched in step with the bier. Mother was crying. This time it was Grandmother's bier ahead. On the emerald-green shawl there were three immense dishes full of ice and sprinklers of rosewater. Four flower vases stood at the corners of the shawl and two between the dishes. The box containing chapters of the Koran stood up in front, where there were lecterns. People were bent over the Koran chapters on the lecterns or in their laps and recited them softly and under their breath. Their heads rose and fell. Above them as they chanted was the chandelier with its forty crystal arms, and in front of them the brass incense burners. In the corner, clear of people, stood funeral lamps hung with glass pendants and feathers. There was not a breath of wind. Were the feathers green and red or black . . .? They were black.

The Prince heard only a hubbub of sound that he could make no sense of. The chandelier did not so much as flicker. They had lit every candle in it. Father did not clasp his hand. The Prince looked at the buttons on his own tunic and said:

'Mother, I want to get down.'

Mother said: 'Well, you're an adult now, my boy' and began to cry.

The Prince was walking beside Murad Khan. Ahead, Father's bier was swaying from side to side. Murad Khan said:

'We all have to go some time, Prince.' He looked down at his boots. 'Your father was a good man, Prince.'

'I know,' said the Prince.

Prince Ehtejab was aware that Grandfather had sat down again in his picture frame and Father was back to trotting on his bay between the hills. The Koran reciters were chanting over one another. The Prince remained standing while the throng came and went. They buried Father at the feet of Grandfather and Grandmother. They were bent over their Koran excerpts, reciting them aloud, while fresh copies were handed out among the crowd. The reciters chanted louder. The aunts had been a long time sitting in their picture frames. There eyes were holes. As for Mother, she was no longer crying. And the Prince coughed.

The door opened and Prince Ehtejab saw those two dark eyes framed by the flower-print prayer chador. The Prince said:

'Where is Fakhronissa?'

The chador opened, revealing a chiselled nose, then rouged cheeks, a smile, teeth and then . . . The Prince said:

'I said, girl, where's Fakhronissa.'

A hand behind the veil twitched it back to frame only the eyes. And those eyes were dark and lively, with glittering pupils. The long shadow of the lashes reached the hem of the chador. A glimpse of two eyebrows, long and luxuriant, a nod in the direction of the head of the staircase, and the Prince found himself having climbed the whole flight of stairs. On the terrace, Fakhronissa was sitting with her back to him, in her pleated lace dress. Two long plaits of hair came down to the delicate folds at her waist. The Prince stood there. He traced out the soft and smooth lines of her shoulders and the shape of her arms appearing faintly through the lace dress. His eyes fell on the back of the chair, and he turned from her silhouette to the whiteness of the back of her neck and the delicate hairs on it. Fakhronissa was seated on her revolving chair. At her elbow was a table. The Prince took in a crystal decanter with a handle, two long-stemmed glasses and two dishes of dried fruits and Isfahan nougat. The carafe was half-full. Fakhronissa still sat with her back to the Prince. He took a step nearer. Beyond the delicate line of her neck and the pleats on her right shoulder, he saw a large leather-bound volume and long white fingers. Fakhronissa laid a finger in the book and shut it. She turned round, and before he was close enough to make out the taunting look through her spectacles, she said:

'Please, sit yourself, Khosrow Khan.'

Prince Ehtejab glanced at the balustrade and the tips of the pine trees beyond it and the pine cones and the spectacles.

'Forgive me for disturbing you, but I couldn't help noticing . . .'

'Indeed, you couldn't help noticing that you were lonely and now that your lady mother has passed on it is time to give a thought to your *fiancée*. Please, sit down.'

The Prince sat down on a chair on the other side of the table.

'So you knew I would come to pay my compliments.'

Fakhronissa clasped the handle of the decanter. As she poured the wine into the glass, the Prince thought he heard again the calling of turtledoves.

'Please. It is our own wine. I believe it must be seven years old. I had it brought from Jalilabad.'

The Prince examined Fakhronissa's delicate features, so like a miniature painting, so near and yet so far away, and the curve of her chin and the white, sculpted neck that extended to the pleats of her lace dress. But when he attempted to trace the swelling of her breasts, as they vanished into the pleats at her chest, Fakhronissa said:

'Please. Time enough for that.'

'Indeed, indeed.'

The Prince drained his glass. The wine was bitter, and as it went down his throat, the Prince felt sweat start on his forehead.

'Seven years old?' said the Prince.

'Yes. It is the very wine that your late mother ordered to be laid down on the day of our betrothal.'

The Prince stared at Fakhronissa's long, white fingers. Four fingers lay on the edge of the table. And the other hand . . .? The Prince realised it was hidden by the heavy folio.

'What are you reading?'

'The memoirs of our common noble ancestor.'

'And you, what do you find to read in these things?'

Once again those long, white fingers that were like five small white fishes closed round the handle of the decanter, and once again the turtledove cooed in his glass.

'Do drink one more glass. The physicians are of the opinion that for haemorrhoids wine is . . .'

And she laughed, so Prince Ehtejab could again see

the two fine dimples each side of her mouth and the row of short, white teeth. He said:

'Haemorrhoids?'

Bitterness flooded his throat. As he unwrapped a piece of nougat from its coloured wrapper, Fakhronissa said:

'You see, if we are to know each other better, we should start with these things here, with these ancestors of ours.'

Fakhronissa lifted up the book and the Prince saw that there was another dimple at the beauty spot on her left cheek, and he sipped his wine.

'Believe me, this great-grandfather of ours cared only for his blessed haemorrhoids. Sometimes they bled or had to be operated on or Dr Abu Nuvas forbade him to ride out or he took a purgative or in his private apartments, hidden from the eyes of his attendants, he enjoyed wine in the hope that his haemorrhoids might give him some respite. It was like that all the time.'

'Well, what's so worth reading about that?'

'I know, but it really is a problem: why were our forebears, every one of them, always thinking of their blessed constitutions, their blessed insides, their blessed haemorrhoids? And if, as it turned out, there was nothing going on down there, and they couldn't find anybody's throat to slit, for example, at your garden gate, why was it they'd be saddled up and off with Chief-Stalker-wallah, Scribe-wallah, Head-Footman-wallah, Valet-wallah, Rifle-Bearer-wallah, Mullah-wallah, Doctor-wallah up hill and down dale to massacre red deer, ibex, black partridge, hare and who knows what else? And why, just as soon as they come exhausted back to camp, must they take a wife for the night? And why, next morning, present one fellow with a robe of honour and cut off another's head and confiscate his estates?'

Prince Ehtejab crossed his legs. He laid his right hand on the edge of the table and counted off his fingers, one by one. Then he lifted up the decanter so he could hear the voice of the turtledove. Fakhronissa said:

'It's a good wine.'

And the Prince again felt the sweat on his forehead. He said:

'Wasn't it that they had nothing to do?'

'Nothing to do? Not a bit of it. This fortunate existence of theirs left not a moment's respite from morning till night. One had to rule several hundreds of thousands of human beings, scribble a minute on all those petitions, knout, decapitate, confiscate vassal property, wear oneself out with toadies and yes-men and parasites, rob them blind, and all without letting go of so much as a penny. Isn't that something to do? To keep a grip on the clergy and the seminary students with their sticks and clubs, who are just biding their time till "His Grace" pronounces your blood can be lawfully shed? To keep busy and happy the Household and Dependants* wriggling about indoors and waiting with bated breath for some eunuch or slave boy to discover he has a bit of man still attached to him? Isn't that something to do? Just imagine, one man and all those virgin maids, all those women with dusky eyes and brows, all those boys just coming into their beards presented as gifts to Your Luminousness! And then those wretched haemorrhoids and bouts of bleeding and that even more wretched Abu Nuvas who has categorically forbidden the *congressus venereus*!'

She looked the Prince over and frowned:

'What about you? How would you have measured up in the race?'

'What race?'

Fakhronissa laughed. She laughed loud. The furrows each side of her lips reached to her sculpted chin. The beauty spot on the left of her mouth vanished in the fine creases.

'My, you are an innocent. Between this great-

* *Utrat wa ismat*: an Arabic euphemism for wives and daughters.

grandfather and all our noble ancestors there was an unusual sort of competition as to who had accounted for the most (a) wives and (b) decapitations. Each one of them was determined to have the more numerous and multifarious harem . . .'

She straightened her spectacles and began to leaf through the book. She glanced at the Prince over her glasses. One of her plaits had fallen onto the left breast . . .

'Shall I read a bit for you?'

The Prince drained his glass, shelled a pistachio and put it in his mouth. Fakhronissa was still looking at him:

'Today we did not feel especially well. The beaters had drawn a comb through the hills. The attendants bade us mount. We found a mount for Dr Abu Nuvas to wait on us. It was brought to our attention that the bear had again been sighted. It was cold. We had forgotten to put on our jerkins and fur topcoats, but we rode on all the same. Alamdar Khan, the chief huntsman, reported that the beaters had driven the bear to ground. We noted that Dr Abu Nuvas was alarmed and ordered him to return to camp. We ourselves set off with attendants for the hill. The Chief Huntsman suggested that we would be advised to dismount. We proceeded on foot. The road climbed. The attendants lagged. Despite our age we were better on the hill than the lot of them. The sons of bitches weren't worthy of our bread

and salt. At last we reached the place and settled down behind a rock. Aga Beik submitted that the bear had gone to ground in a certain cave. We took cover behind a wild almond tree. The attendants came up. Their faces were drained of colour. Aga Beik tossed a firecracker into the cave, which was about ten feet from us. The bear came out. It was vast. We had never bagged such a bear before. We hit him with a good blast of buckshot from our French 15-gauge, in the head, and he rolled over. The attendants broke into wild congratulation. There and then Aga Beik presented me with a horse and a Russian rifle. It was a good hunting trip. We gave orders that the bear should be skinned and the pelt sent to Fakhrosultaneh. When we were back under canvas, Alamdar Khan reported that the bear had still had some life in him and had mauled one of the attendants. The huntsmen had bagged thirty-five red deer, twenty to thirty hares and two ibex. One of the stags was fifteen years old. Muqtaderolmulk was very proud of himself. We gave instructions that the Russian hunting-piece be given to him. We took luncheon under an awning. There was an uproar coming from the ladies' tents. Hajebadowleh came and reported that the women were quarrelling about the bear skin.

'In the afternoon, we felt ghastly. Dr Abu Nuvas administered an infusion. The damn fellow has been eating his head off at my expense for ten years and still has no idea. Fakhrosultaneh sent word that this evening she would expect the

honour of our visit. She's a fine girl, but a bit too full of herself.
We sent back that she was not to expect us. That was for the sake
of peace among the women. Ibrahim Beik lit a bunch of wild rue
and twirled the smoke round our head. He said that our Blessed
Person must have been touched by the evil eye. We roared with
laughter. He's a good man to have in attendance.'

Fakhronissa took off her spectacles. She shut the book, though her finger stayed between the pages:

'You can see how much you have to catch up. Great-grandfather would certainly have spent that night with a new girl, maybe even a Georgian . . .'

The Prince said: 'These hunting expeditions were nothing much to talk about. From twelve feet, loaded with buckshot, any fool can . . .'

Fakhronissa laughed: 'And the girls, what about them?'

Fakhri was standing at the door of the terrace, with those eyes framed by the flower-print dark chador.

'Madame, lunch is served.'

Fakhronissa said: 'You go on. We are coming straight away.'

Fakhri turned round, and the Prince stared at her shoulders and her waist and the flowing curves of her bottom. Her prayer chador hugged her figure. Fakhronissa said:

'Fakhri is still a virgin. Would you like me to present her to Your Excellency so you can get started? Although I know you won't make any sort of showing in the Ancestral Challenge.'

The Prince said: 'She's a pretty girl.'

Fakhronissa said: 'Only her eyes are pretty. And doesn't she know it herself!'

And she poured herself some wine and drained it in one. She put the book on the side of the table and her spectacles on top. The Prince looked into Fakhronissa's eyes. Her eyes, too, were dark. But she did not blink. Her pupils were washed out.

'Your eyes are pretty as well.'

Fakhronissa poured some wine out also for the Prince. 'Nothing worth the mention. This particular horse is not worth running. A gift-horse makes a better mount.'

The Prince touched the white and elongated hand that lay on the book. Fakhronissa said: 'You should know that if you want to win the race, you don't waste time with sweet nothings. You shouldn't beat about the bush.'

With her right hand she tossed back a tress of hair. The Prince stared at her cleavage and the curve of her two breasts, which were small and round. He took her hand.

'What about Grandfather?'

'He wasted his time. Each day one should cut off only one or two heads, and shoot only two or three stags and ibex so that by the evening one can still ride a couple of gift-horses or vice versa. What one mustn't do is become attached to any one of these things, come to depend on it. Grandfather came to depend on something, and that was the sight of blood. He had a taste for the colour of blood. He had even given the order that the hilt of his sword be inlaid with rubies, immense rubies. One or two splashes of blood, maybe, to regulate the bowels, but if it must be more, if one becomes inured to it, if it becomes a race one has to win, well, that should not be.'

The Prince drank off his wine and looked at the flush in Fakhronissa's cheeks. Fakhronissa began to fidget with her spectacles and the leather binding of the book.

'Well, the way you tell it, at least in one department Grandfather . . .'

'No, in neither of them. He failed in both contests. You see that was his mistake. You must win both or you'll lose both. When you cut a fellow's head off, whatever happens you must take his daughter or his niece or one of his womenfolk to bed so there are no hard feelings. Then if she's the sort of girl that's forever in tears, is covered head to foot in black, doesn't want to do

70

it, tries to get away, even scrapes the make-up from her face and messes up her hair, it's easier to manage her. You see how simple the whole thing is. Because of course this girl will all the time be terrified that one just might lose patience and cry out, "Master Executioner!" or have them take her brother, who has just become *valet de chambre*, tie him up and beat the soles of his feet. Grandfather wore himself into the ground. For all that he was loathed, he was a nobody, just a provincial governor that his father could drop in the bat of an eyelid. That is why he was in such a tearing hurry. He wanted to achieve in fifteen years what his forebears had needed twenty, thirty, even fifty years to accomplish. He poisoned his guests in batches, pulled the roofs down on the heads of entire tribal dynasties. And then because he was tired in the evening, he couldn't mount his gift-horses, and the horses naturally turned skittish and lashed out. He fell prey to remorse and the mood could last a full week.'

She stood up: 'Would you like to hear something about Grandfather's fits of remorse.'

'No,' said the Prince, 'I mean, if you will excuse me.'

'It won't take me a moment to find, and besides, it will be good for your appetite. These bouts of regret and remorse worked as a sort of powerful purge on his blessed insides, so he could go back to it with his old gusto.'

Her white dress came down to her feet. Her plaits lay one on each breast. As she stepped into the hall, the Prince examined her white nape, the curve of her shoulders and her waist. He looked at the lees at the bottom of his glass and then into Fakhronissa's face. She was seated again on her swivel chair, leafing through Grandfather's book of memoirs, and eyeing the Prince from under her lashes, but not laughing any more.

'It'll take a moment to find. You're not bored, are you?'

The Prince poured himself some wine. The wine was deep red in colour. The glass ran over and wine spilled on the oilcloth. The red wine flowed like a tiny canal to the edge of the table. The Prince looked at the red droplets that dripped from the edge of the table, poured himself some more, continued to look. As he put the empty decanter on the table, Fakhronissa said:

'If you'd like, I'll have some more brought. We have a whole cask.'

The Prince said: 'No, I'll never be anything in this game.'

He drank his wine. After each sip, he studied the wine and the lees that had collected on the bottom. Fakhronissa read out: '*In truth, Isfahan today is like Balkh of old, which was known as the "Dome of Islam". Apart from the clerics and mullahs and reciters of holy tales and the preachers . . .'*

She glanced at the Prince: 'No, it's not here. Still . . .'

She turned the pages. And the Prince knew that in all that thick folio, it wasn't there: that Grandfather had forgotten even the name of Munireh Khatun. And he allowed Munireh Khatun to return to life in all her warm and living fleshiness. And Munireh Khatun lifted Khosrow up and pressed him to her bosom. Her breasts were warm. Laughing, she said:

'Do you like that, Khosrow Khan?'

The Prince put his arms round Munireh Khatun's neck. Munireh Khatun's palms were sweaty. She gripped his knees and rubbed them against her breast.

'Do you like that, Khosrow Khan?'

She rubbed harder. Munireh Khatun's body was fleshy and warm. The Prince put his arms tighter round her neck. He had his head back and was staring into Munireh Khatun's eyes. Munireh Khatun's hair spread over her shoulders. She had leaned back against the wall. Then she stroked him with her hand. The Prince shuddered. He felt her body had become naked. Munireh Khatun's plump and sweaty fingers went on stroking him.

'Do you like it? Do you like it?'

The Prince did not like it at all. From the room on the other side he heard the voice of the Ladies' Chaplain, who loud and long was reciting the story of the Passion of Hussein.* He heard Grandmother, Mother and the other ladies sobbing away in the main saloon. Grandmother had said: 'Don't budge from here!' But Khosrow had run off. Munireh Khatun was in her own sitting-room. She had put on her black prayer chador. Only her dark eyes were visible. She said:

'Have you come to play with me again, Khosrow Khan?'

Munireh Khatun threw off her black chador, took Khosrow Khan by the hand, and went into the storeroom. Light came in through a skylight.

She said: 'Do you like this?' and sat down. The Prince sat down on Munireh Khatun's huge thighs. His legs were between two mountains of flesh. Munireh Khatun continued to stroke him and said:

'Do you like it?'

* The death in battle of the Prophet's grandson Hussein at Kerbela on October 10, 680 led to the schism in Islam between the mainstream *Sunni* and the *Shia*, which predominates in Iran. It is a favourite subject in Iranian drama and story-telling.

The Prince's head lay between the warm, perspiring breasts of Munireh Khatun. Those breasts were trembling. Her breathing quickened. She lay down on her back. The Prince felt hot. He said:

'I want to go. I'm not playing any more. I don't like it. I don't like it.'

Munireh Khatun said: 'Don't you want to ride horsey bareback, eh?'

The light fell on to her neck. The Prince's hands rested on the trembling mounds of Munireh Khatun's damp breasts. Munireh Khatun said:

'Just a bit more! A wee bit more!'

'I don't want to,' said the Prince. 'I don't like it.' And he shouted out: 'GRANDMOTHER!'

Munireh Khatun got to her feet. Her hands were trembling. The Prince stared at her breasts. Her hair was strewn over her shoulders. 'Hang on! Let me get my clothes on!'

Her hands shook.

'Where have you been?' said Grandmother.

The Prince sat down. Mother leaned forward. The voice of the Ladies' Chaplain came at them.

'I was playing with Munireh Khatun. We were playing horsey.'

Grandmother said: 'The slut! Again she . . .'

'What happened, Forugh Sultan?' asked Older Aunt.

'Absolutely nothing.'

Younger Aunt took Khosrow by the hand. 'Come and sit by me, Khosrow.'

Grandmother held on. 'No. Stay here, Khosrow.'

The Ladies' Chaplain's voice was loud and drawn out. Grandmother drew on the mouthpiece of her water pipe. From one end of the room to the other were seated women. Younger Aunt still pulled at Khosrow's hand. The Prince pulled back. Older Aunt stood up and went away. The other women rose. Only Mother remained seated, and Grandmother. Grandmother said under her breath:

'At last, she's gone!'

And she blew out the smoke. Younger Aunt came nearer. The Prince moved closer to Grandmother. Younger Aunt said:

'Was he with Munireh Khatun again, Forugh Sultan?'

The women were crying. Grandmother bowed at the waist. Younger Aunt bowed. The Prince heard only the voice of the Ladies' Chaplain and saw his shadow on the curtain. Also the shadow of his water pipe. Nanny Ghamar bowed and said:

'His Highness orders . . .'

Grandmother said: 'Just as soon as the Sheikh has finished, it will be done.'

Nanny Ghamar sat down and picked up the water pipe. Her eyelids were white. A few grey hairs could be seen under her headscarf. The Prince heard Grandfather's loud and gruff voice:

'Forugh Sultan!'

Fakhronissa was still leafing through the book. The Prince cried out:

'Her screams could be heard in the garden, believe me, even as far as the trees and the gate. They must have used a branding iron on her. Laleh Aga the tutor said so.'

But Fakhronissa was just a silhouette: like those women in miniature that stretched around the walls of the great hall, standing beneath a weeping willow or seated by a stream with hair unbound, wine-cup in hand. Fakhronissa was holding a book, that same great leather-bound volume, and read out:

'By God, it was not my fault. My father had issued an order and because I wanted no taint of suspicion that I was making up to the Paramount Chief of the Qashqai, I did what I should never have done. It was Father's express order and it is written, "Obey those set in authority over you."* At times I thought I'd do

* Koran 4:59.

away with myself and be free of the whole thing. But I knew that canon law forbids self-murder, and I would be in trouble both in this world and the next. God and His Prophet are my witnesses that one day I said to Sayyid Habib, "Saddle my mount", and we went out together into the country. I handed him the revolver and entreated him, "For the love of your ancestor Zohreh,* put me out of my misery." Sayyid Habib wept and said, "What are you saying?" I said, "Tomorrow, what am I to say to your forebear the Prophet? How can I look him in the face? I can face retribution here below. Do as I ask so that haply God will take the guilt from my head."

'He spoke: "For all the blood on his hands, Hajjaj bin Yusef † still hoped for God's mercy." He kissed my hand and my knee, tried to prostrate himself but I would not let him. I kissed him on the face. On the way back we killed two hares with birdshot. The Sayyid told a story he'd read I don't know where that one day Hajjaj gives a few pence to a beggar and said, "Pray for me." So the beggar prays for him every evening. Hajjaj dies and one night appears to the beggar in a dream, asks him: "Why aren't you praying for me?" Beggar says: "I thought it was all up with you and my prayers wouldn't do any good." Hajjaj says, "Thanks to

---

* Fatimeh Zohreh was the daughter of the Prophet and famed for her sanctity. A Sayyid is a descendant of the Prophet's family, hence 'ancestor'.

† Umayyad Governor of Baghdad and archetypal tyrant.

you, many of my sins were wiped from the slate." The beggar asks:
"So there is still hope?" And he says, "Assuredly. Keep praying!"'

Fakhronissa was still seated on her chair with the book in her hand, and her spectacles on. The Prince said:

'I said: "I want to see her, Laleh Aga." He said: "Get on with your recitation." I said: "But I want to." He said: "Alright, so long as there's no crying." I said: "I won't cry." He said: "When Mullah Hussein goes, then alright. But just one minute. Understood?" "Understood," I said.

'Her sitting-room was bare. The carpet had been rolled up and laid against the wall. I could hear a faint, but continuous whimpering.

'"Aren't you scared at all?"

'"No."

'He took my hand. He was very tall. The sound was coming from behind the door of the storeroom. Laleh Aga pulled back the bolt. I could see only a column of light and the white of Munireh Khatun's face. Her eyelids were closed. I said: "Laleh Aga, why have they shaved her head?" He said: "Have you had your look?" Her dress was in tatters. Her heavy breasts were showing. They had tied her hands to two tether stakes. Her feet were in stocks. She was whimpering. Laleh Aga said: "Have your look and then let's go." He had said that out loud. The eyelids opened and Munireh Khatun turned her head. Her hands shook. The light fell on her bare arms. She said: "Is that you, Khosrow Khan? Have you come to play with me?" She laughed. Her breasts heaved as she laughed.

'I said: "I'm scared, Laleh Aga."

'Laleh Aga grasped my hand.

'Munireh Khatun cried out: "Have you come to play with me, Khosrow Khan? Do you want to play bareback horsey, eh? To get up on Munireh Khatun, the lawful wedded wife of His Royal Highness? Do you want to?" She laughed.

'Laleh Aga shut the storeroom door. She went on laughing, loud. Laleh Aga said: "I told you so. She's crazy." I said: "Why?" He said: "They branded her. They held her by the arms and branded her with a red-hot iron."'

Prince Ehtejab had his head bowed, resting on his two hands. Why did I burn the photograph of Great-grandfather? Grandfather had written: '*Master Habib is a true blood descendant of the Prophet. He often gave me sound advice. He spoke of the ocean of God's Grace and reminded me that* He that obeys orders bears no blame.' Munireh Khatun must have screamed and begged him, 'Have mercy on me, Prince, I did wrong.' Grandfather must have stood under the willow-tree. Or perhaps the rambling rose? He looked on. He had instructed the servants to give Sayyid Habib a Kashmir shawl and forty gold pieces. He had written: '*May God lengthen his days. Sayyid Habib is a man of fine sensibility.*'

The Prince asked: 'Madame Fakhronissa, what about Father?'

'Now your father could have won the race. In just one hour or two, he brought to nothing what your noble ancestors had needed years to create. It's quite something with just one order to crush a whole boulevard of people under the wheels and tracks of tanks and armoured cars. You used to say that yourself. Shame that he quit so early.'

And the Prince saw that Fakhronissa was becoming as remote and strange as the photograph. He saw there was dust on her black hair. He began to cough. As his shoulders shook with the coughing and he saw that he was no longer able . . . then he understood that he must begin anew, that whatever the consequence, he must . . . and he said out loud:

'From where?'

He burst out coughing again. Fakhri laid the table, then went into her room, turned on the light and sat down in front of the looking glass. She combed her hair, bunched it and let it fall over her right shoulder. She drew out a few bangs over her forehead and looked into the mirror. She studied her plump, red lips, then combed her hair again and let it fall over her left shoulder. She stood up, turned her back on the mirror and tried to examine the back of her neck. But since some of her hair still fell on her back, she picked up a hand mirror, put it behind her head and sat down again. She cast her hair over her right shoulder. The nape of her neck was white and pleasant-looking. The same two fine lines as on her mistress' neck. Amidst her black tresses she came upon a white hair. She tried to pull it out, without success, till she took up a handful and dug the white hair out.

The Prince coughed. Fakhri pulled open a drawer, riffled through her mistress' make-up, picked out her mistress' little folding mirror, and opened it. On one side was a picture of her mistress and Prince Ehtejab. They were standing one beside the other. The Prince's hair was sparse. Madame's hair was thick and black. She wiped the glass and could see her mistress' beauty spot and even the two soft dimples at the corners of her mouth and the weak eyes behind the glass of her spectacles. When I tried to wear the glasses, O what a scene he'd made! He said: 'I told you to be Fakhronissa, but not down to every tic . . .' The Prince was purple as a mulberry, grabbed the glasses and threw them in among Madame's make-up things.

She rummaged in the drawer. The spectacles were where they were every evening. She put them on and looked in the mirror. Her eyes were still bright unlike Fakhronissa, who never blinked her eyelids, always nose in a book, from sundown to midnight. In the day, too. Even when she was sitting before her looking glass and I was combing her hair. She used to say: 'Fakhri love, let the hair fall over my shoulder, not like that', and go back to reading. Only her lips moved. I'd say: 'What's it say there, Ma'am?' She'd say: 'Would you like me to read it to you?' 'Oh yes,' I said and she read the story of the Castle of Raining Stones.* I said: 'Madame, that's all lies.'

'I know,' she said, 'but I wanted to hear the sort of thing my noble ancestors dozed off to.'

She wiped the photograph with Fakhri's gown. Fakhronissa was laughing. Prince Ehtejab frowned. Same old story. But that evening how he roared! What a nerve! There in the presence of the dead. I was so scared.

She brought the picture over to the mirror and looked at herself. If only my face were a little slimmer. If only the Prince would let me put these glasses on. He's always saying: 'Your eyesight is still good.' He used to put a pen between my fingers and press down. He'd say: 'I'm your

* A story by Naqibolmamalik, court story-teller to the Nassereddin Shah Qajar at the end of the nineteenth century.

private tutor.' Why can't he have children? With Fakhronissa he couldn't have a child either.

She brought her face forward and looked at the neck in the photograph and then at her own neck. The Prince is always saying, 'Your neck would be just like Fakhronissa's, if only a little bit . . .' Nothing I can do about it. What he really likes is to put his face between one's tits and in a moment he's asleep. I keep saying, 'Prince lovey, I can't breathe. That's enough', but he takes not the slightest notice. He's always saying: 'Grandfather took a virgin girl to bed with him every night.' He says: 'I'm not a man any more. If I were, I wouldn't stand to put up with just you alone.' Not a man any more, he says, but he wants it every night. And then he lays his head between my tits and falls asleep. I say: 'Dear Prince, I have to sleep as well.' What with all the housework to do and me all on my own. If I try to get up early and get down to it, he says: 'Fakhronissa used to lie in till noon.' Very well, I want to lie in as well. Then who's going to do all the housework? How did a prince end up with me? I say, I say: 'Prince, please marry me? If I get pregnant, I'll be in big trouble?' He only says: 'Fakhronissa, you should be ashamed of yourself!' But I'm not Fakhronissa. I'm Fakhri. Thank God he can't have children. What would I do with a bastard out of wedlock? But things like that just don't occur to people like him.

She looked at the photograph and then at her own face and painted the beauty spot just by the left corner of her mouth. The Prince said: 'Put the beauty spot on the left side of your lips, not on your peasant's gob.' Then he hit me.

She darkened the beauty spot. She laughed just like the photograph and saw the crease at the corner of her mouth run through it. As she studied the photograph, she combed her hair. She leaned forward: 'If he spies just a single white hair . . .'

But she did not find a single white hair. She stood the photograph by the full-length mirror. She undid her apron and put it in the pocket of her dress. Her headscarf was in her apron pocket. If only my waist were a little bit slimmer . . . Whatever I do it doesn't seem to work. These eyes of mine . . . If only the beauty spot never washed off. When Madame was reading, she used to burst out laughing.

The Prince said: 'Read it out loud.'

'But I can't read or write,' I said.

He said: 'I'll teach you.'

She stood up and went over to the chest of drawers. She touched the dresses. Every one of them was of white lace. Why can't he once in a while buy me another dress? I'm just sick and tired.

She took out one of the dresses, stepped in front of the mirror, held it in front of her and looked in the mirror. Then she bent down and looked at the photograph. Every one of them with a scalloped neckline, like Madame's dress, the one that she . . . The blood from the corner of her mouth was dripping onto the fine bed sheet and the stain spread wider and wider . . . I said: 'Please, Prince dear, it's not nice in front of the dead!' The Prince turned my face to him and nibbled at my lip. I turned away again. Madame's body shuddered under the sheet. How thin she was! I screamed. The Prince said: 'On the contrary, it's nice like this.' He had a nerve, the Prince!

She laid the white lace dress on the arm of the chair and took her own dress off. Her bare arms were plump and white. She bent down, folded her dress and put it in the iron chest in the corner. She closed the hasp. Dawn till dusk I have to sweep, I'm sick and tired of it.

She stood in front of the mirror and examined her arms, her bosom and her cleavage and the beauty spot at the corner of her mouth and the hank of dark hair tumbling onto her shoulders. He's always laying his head on my breast. He never did that with Fakhronissa. Why did he say, It's nice like this, go on, scream, scream?

She put on the dress and straightened the spectacles on her nose. The dress now fitted her like a glove. Only at the shoulder was it a little tight, and it squeezed at her breasts. She straightened the collar and tossed her hair over the left shoulder and breast. How did Madame manage always to have her hair on the left breast? She used to sit and read. I once said: 'Prince, I also want to read books.' 'Fine,' he said. 'I'll be your private tutor.' Those books were all about Great-grandfather or Heaven knows who.

She took her belt in her hand. This damn waist of mine.

She put on the belt and sat down on the chair. She bowed her neck. She took up the little mirror, examined herself in it and squinted at her mistress, who now stood upside down beside the Prince. With her hand she smoothed her hair, but she saw it was again dishevelled, and she combed it once more, thinking: On a bed like this you can sleep like a top, stretch out your legs and stare at the ceiling. You can look at the plasterwork flower patterns and that wee angel peeping out of the petunia and the tiny mirrors all over the place. Why is one of his wings broken?

She inspected her beauty spot. Madame used to say, 'I don't have any faith. That sort of thing is all very well for ordinary folk, or people who must slave away from dawn to dusk, and then in the evening have nowhere to lay their heads.' If only the Prince would get up and we could go in to dinner. The food will get cold. The Prince at one end and me at the other. Why can't he have children? I would have liked ten, boys and girls, all pretty, like . . .

Her neck was still bent. Her silky hair gleamed in the mirror: yes, a headscarf is a blessing also for these sorts of situation, keeps dust out of one's hair and . . . The Prince said: 'Let Fakhri do the slaving, not you!' Well, that really is what some people have to put up with. But why did he burn the books?

She had strained her eyes and could no longer distinguish things in the gloom. Her cleavage, at least, and the beauty spot she could see. Why won't he get up? What on earth is wrong with him this evening? God forbid that . . .

When she laughed, she saw the creases deepen at the corners of her mouth. However hard she looked, she could not see the beauty spot in the creases. The contours of her face kept blurring. Her hair was a dark mass that flowed all the way down to her left breast. The eyes stared without blinking from behind the thick glass of the spectacles and could, at last, there in the mirror, amid the blurred, flowing, trembling contours, make out her mistress Fakhronissa. If only I'd had a baby! I was always saying, 'Can't you at least get a daily woman for all the housework?' He said: 'Fakhri can manage.' 'All on her own?' 'She can manage. I know she can.' He stroked my hair and said, 'Fakhronissa, don't you be putting on airs.'

She had her neck straight and her breasts plumped up. If he had got a daily, someone who . . . all these dishes . . . and I all on my own . . .

She snapped the little mirror shut, put it in the drawer and closed it. She laid her hands on the arms of the chair and leaned back. If only he would come downstairs. In this house, how could one keep a daily, what with the work and him such a nag? Not to mention that he likes to lie in wait in the kitchen or behind the door, and when Fakhri comes through with a tray in her hands, pinches her bottom or puts a hand down the poor girl's front . . .?

She said out loud: 'Really, Prince, it's disgusting, you at your age and in your position.'

The Prince said: 'Great-grandfather had a hundred wives, wedded or temporary, a hundred, and every night a new one. Imagine that, Fakhronissa, and that's not counting the dancing-girls. And here I am with just you . . .'

The Prince coughed and heard the stained glass rattle.

Fakhronissa said: 'And what on earth has that to do with the present and with a female servant in the house? A prince, they'll say, and a housemaid, they'll say. What if they get to hear of it, those half-blood cousins on your father's side and those full-blood *cousines* on your mother's side?'

'To hell with them all,' said the Prince.

He went on: 'You are aware, Fakhronissa, that Grandfather gave the order to brand Munireh Khatun. They pressed a red-hot branding iron to the place where...'

Fakhri said: 'How was I to know that? In these books there's nothing about it, and anyway my reading isn't...'

The Prince said: 'I can still hear her scream. With a red-hot branding iron, Fakhronissa! I bet Grandfather said: "Now the rest of them will think twice about what they're up to."'

And he burst out coughing. Fakhri was still seated in front of the mirror, thinking: At that time, she pretended not to know what was going on. She just looked at me through her spectacles.

She squinted. Her mistress was sittting in the mirror, staring at one, in the way she had, from out of the corners of her glasses. With her white handkerchief she wiped the glass of the mirror. The contours of her body swam. I did say: 'Prince, once when I went upstairs with the tea tray, Madame said . . .'

'Your maid,' the Prince said.

I went on: 'She said, Fakhri, do you also get fun out of it.' I said: 'No, Ma'am.' She said: 'Well, why do you laugh in that raucous way?' I said: 'Because he stuffs his hand down my front.' She said: 'Have you been to bed with him?' 'No, Ma'am,' I said.

She stared hard and without blinking into the mirror. She saw a couple of soft lines on her forehead.

She said: 'It's disgusting, Fakhri. At the very least . . .' She had said that out loud. She reached out her hand to take a glass from the silver tray. As if it was my fault, if the Prince wanted it, and Madame wasn't interested, just sat there all the time . . . Why was she so thin? Her arms were like two sticks. And so white.

The hand stayed in mid-air. The tea tray was with Fakhri, dressed in her apron and headscarf, over there in the darkness. She reached out her hand, took a pair of earrings and put them on. The earrings glittered. She turned her head. She peered at the left earring. They look nice on me, too!

She ran her fingers over her mass of hair and let it fall onto her cleavage. She took out the necklace as well. It was heavy. If only he had got somebody to do the housework . . . I'm just not up to it. I'm always having to wash! Now Madame, how pale her body was! Just skin and bone. Her breasts were little, white and round. Her tummy . . .

The necklace rested on her hair as far as her cleavage. She fingered each pearl, one by one. Madame hadn't cared for it at all. She had so much jewellery, a mother-of-pearl box full of it. She used to sit in front of the mirror and put on one necklace after another. She used to say: 'Fakhri love, do see if this suits me?'

She said out loud. 'It suits me too. Really nicely.'

She was saying: 'Fakhri, my love, you go to bed. I'll wait up. I suppose he's stayed up at the tables somewhere.' I said: 'I'll wait up with you, Ma'am.'

She looked through the corner of her eye at the stove at the end of the room, half of it visible in the mirror, and said:

'I'll wait till dawn, till the Prince . . .'

She took out the bracelets and put them on one by one. They are still too tight. These fingers of mine! Madame's fingers were elongated and white. As for her fingernails . . . But then when one has to do all these dishes from morning till night . . .

She said: 'If only he'd taken on somebody.'

She looked at the glitter of the bracelets in the mirror and at the place by the stove where Fakhri was still standing behind her mistress' head. The Prince was standing in the darkness and was running his cold hands over Fakhri's naked body. Very slowly I went up to him, placed my hand on his shoulder and said: 'Prince, this is disgraceful. At least act like your great-grandfather, and marry her.' The Prince turned round. He was kissing Fakhri's neck. He had put his arm round my waist, that is, round Fakhri's waist, and said: 'I can't have children, Fakhronissa.' I said: 'Well, take her at least to bed. Here isn't the place for it.' The Prince said: 'Alright. Be patient a moment, will you?' I left the room. They were still in the corner, in the darkness, entwined.

And she said: 'What is that to me, who . . .?'

She stared. She held her neck upright. Madame's lips when she had no lipstick on were so white! Her teeth too were white. And fine.

She picked up a pink lipstick and applied it to her lips. I must wait up, even if he doesn't come home till morning. If he hadn't burned the books, I might have done like Madame and . . . The Prince said: 'Fakhronissa, you have come on well. Now you can take on Great-grandfather's *Memoirs* . . .' When Madame was tired, she used to go over to the window, rest her elbows on the windowsill and look out. It was dark outside. The scent of pine and jasmine came in from the garden.

She said out loud: 'You go to bed, Fakhri, my love.'

Fakhri was standing in that corner, out of sight behind her. She had her hands in the pocket of her apron and was looking at the slim shoulders of her mistress, Fakhronissa. Why did she used to look at me in that way at the baths? At my hands, at my feet? She used to stare at my little, white, round breasts. When she combed my hair, she would say: 'How soft you hair is, Ma'am!' I used to say: 'Fakhri, do take care, don't pull my hair out.'

She reached out and touched her hair. It was soft. She stood up. There was now no longer any scent of pines, no scent of jasmine flowers. It was all gone to seed. Why had he sold that house? He said one day to Haidar Ali the gardener, my daddy: 'Be off with you. I don't want you touching the geraniums . . .' He used to come home late. I always had to wait up until the Prince came home drunk. He always sounded his horn. Haidar Ali the gardener and his wife were in bed. I used to go and open the door. The Prince would stick his head out of the car window and say: 'Fakhronissa, my darling, are you still up? You must have been reading. In contrast, I have gambled away that sixth share I owned of the village of Sarutaqi.' Then he would laugh and say: 'Oh, it's you, is

94

it, Fakhri? So where's your mistress?' Why did he always call me Fakhronissa? Fakhronissa was seated at the window, breathing in the scent of pine and jasmine. As the Prince got out, she would grip him under the armpits. The Prince would lay his head on Fakhri's shoulder. They'd go up the stairs together. The Prince would put his arm round my waist, round Fakhri's waist. How his breath stank! His head was burning. I used to wipe the sweat from his forehead. On the landing, Murad would take the Prince under the arms and bring him upstairs. Their shadows fell on the steps. The Prince almost fell. Murad would say: 'Prince, the horses . . . the carriages . . .' and the Prince would say: 'To hell with them, to hell with them!' The Prince would say: 'Murad Khan, who has died of late?' If only I could again look out of the window and breathe the scent of pine and box. All there is now is two tubs of geraniums, and a single willow, and a house with these high walls. Why did the Prince sell the other house? I can't manage it all on my own. Haidar Ali the gardener he threw out, along with his wife and two children. He said: 'This house doesn't need a gardener.' Haidar Ali said: 'Prince, I've served this family for forty years. Where can I go now?' The Prince said: 'To the boneyard.' Haidar Ali said: 'What about my daughter, at least, Prince?' The Prince said: 'Fakhri is dead, Haidar Ali. Fakhri is dead.' The little garden is now full of weeds. They reach half-way up the willow tree. Not even a single carnation stem! Nothing but these little yellow flowers. If it weren't for the two waterlilies and the bindweed twined round the willow . . . He won't even let me change the water in the pool. He says: 'I like the water green like this.' One by one the goldfish died. Every day a crow takes one. When I see the fish floating with their white bellies up and the others circling round, I begin to cry. One day I got up early to change the water in the pool myself. All that water. The plug was stuck fast. All on my own, a poor woman all on her own, I poured bucket after bucket of water onto the garden. I collected the fish in a pan. So many fish there were! The Prince shouted from a window: 'Didn't I tell you that I didn't want . . .' And he started up the pump and filled the pool. When he goes out, he locks the door behind him. At least he could bring somebody to keep me company. Now if Fakhri were here . . .

She stood up, shut the door of her room behind her and went upstairs. Why was he always saying: 'Murad Khan, who's died of late?' It's not as if the Prince had anybody. Apart from a few paternal cousins and maternal *cousines* both full- and half-blood. And anyway for years on end he'd see nothing of them. He never once took me out. How he used to laugh! My throat burned. It tasted bitter. I said: 'Prince, I can't drink it.' He said: 'Fakhronissa, you must drink.' And hit me. He always slapped, with the back of his hand, always on the face, this side. My forehead began to burn, then my hands. The Prince said: 'Have another drink, Fakhronissa.' I said: 'I don't want to.' He glared at me. I was frightened. Why had he become so thin? Like a spindle. I drank. My throat again caught fire. The Prince's head was shaking. He went over to the other side of the table, sat down on his chair and said:

'You must drink it in sips.'

He had a drink and I drank with him. The Prince, how far away he was! All three chandeliers had been lowered and swung to and fro. He said: 'Fakhronissa, I said: Drink!' Now I really wanted to and reached out for the long-stemmed glass which was still half-full. I missed, tried again, raised it. It was cold. It was bitter. But it warmed one up. The Prince was miles away. I was seeing him as if through the waters of a pool. The waters rippled.

He gripped the balustrade and lifted himself up. How he would laugh! I began to cry. He said: 'Fakhronissa, cry away, it'll do you good. But drink the rest of it.' I said: 'I don't want to, my head . . .' He shouted: 'YOU MUST

DRINK.' I said: 'No, I won't.' He stood up. He wasn't a big man. He raised his hand. His face came closer and closer. The waters of the pool broke into waves. He gripped my head and poured the stuff in my mouth, but it spilled onto my breast and onto my dress. I said: 'Prince dear, my dress!' He said. 'To hell with it! There's another . . .' I said: 'I don't like wearing these dresses. Can't you at least buy me another dress, in another style.' He said: 'You can put on Fakhri's dress and tie her scarf round your head.' I said: 'No, I can't. My hands are worn to the bone with all this housework.'

The Prince was sitting in his armchair. He had his head in his hands. He knew that Fakhronissa was now listening at the door and he coughed. The door opened and Fakhronissa switched on the light. Why does he always sit in this room?

The Prince stamped his foot. 'Didn't I tell you not to come upstairs, Fakhri?'

His head was still in his hands. Fakhri could even smell the dust he had raised. What's he doing in this room?

She switched off the light. The room was dark again. Why has he hung up those pictures? Fakhronissa had stuck a carnation in the corner of her mouth. And now the garden's all overgrown. With those little yellow flowers. It'd be nice to put a waterlily in the corner of my mouth.

She had shut the door and was standing on the stairs. What's eating him this evening? Nothing at all on his breath. He hasn't touched any arak for ages. Shame, because it makes one all warm, and one can be Fakhronissa without so much as lifting a finger.

She came down the stairs two at a time and went into the dining-room. It's good at least that he didn't sell the chandeliers and the carpet. What a lot of bird-pattern* china bowls! There were bowls and cups and flower vases on the mantelpiece. That mirrored marquetry bowl with the central medallion. The silver filigree inkstand. Fakhronissa used to say: 'Those are turquoises.' The Jew said: 'Prince, for the chandeliers, now, I have a good buyer.'

She said out loud: 'To hell with him.'

She sat down at the table. Across from her, on the far side of the table, the Prince's chair was empty. I must have something to eat. I can't manage all this on my own and on an empty stomach.

She helped herself to food. All this food, what do we want with it? He's always saying: 'That's not for you to

* *Morghi* or 'bird-pattern' is the Persian name for a nineteenth-century Cantonese export ware much prized in Iran and Central Asia.

worry about.' If he came home, I'd sit down opposite him. If he didn't . . . In the kitchen I can't keep anything down.

She spread a napkin in her lap. How beautifully Madame used to eat! Very slowly. With her long, white fingers, she held her fork and spoon, took just a little from each dish. She drank off her long-stemmed glass in little sips. I never saw her tipsy. She used to say: 'Prince, have a thought for your old age, for I won't be around.' The Prince said: 'Great-grandfather's estate was vast. For all that Grandfather and Father tried, they couldn't quite run through it all.' Fakhronissa said: 'So you are planning to . . .?' The Prince said: 'Yes.' Fakhronissa said: 'At the tables as well?' The Prince said: 'It's the only way.' Fakhronissa said: 'Can't you at least enjoy a virgin or two . . .' The Prince said: 'That's not my thing.' I said: 'Prince, why not at least take on a cleaning-woman?' The Prince said: 'So what's Fakhri supposed to be doing? And how many are we, anyway?' I said: 'Yes, but all alone . . .' The Prince said: 'She'll manage. You don't bother about her, just drink your wine.' I said: 'And on Judgement Day . . .' He cried: 'That's all rubbish! Just drink your wine, Fakhronissa.'

She took a sip of her wine. It had come to taste better. I couldn't bear to go even one evening without it.

Again, she drank. The Prince said: 'Drink it slowly. Then it'll have an effect.'

She took another sip. I can't do it. He drinks so fast and I must . . . If only he'd take on a gardener, then the water in the pool could also . . .

Prince Ehtejab had taken hold of his glass. The wine was a deep red and the lees had collected at the bottom. The chandeliers had come down almost to the table top. And Fakhri – No, Fakhronissa – was broken into pieces by the drops of coloured crystal. Only her eyes were visible. Those same eyes that had been framed by her black chador. Dark and alive.

The long-stemmed glass was empty. She poured out more. The more I said: 'Fakhri love, when the Prince plays around with you, don't laugh so loud.' The girl couldn't care less, with her thick waist and fat arse. She just went on cackling. And when the Prince used to come home at midnight, he'd always go off into Fakhri's room, creep into that shabby bed and start cuddling Fakhri. He'd put Fakhri's arms round his neck and bury his head in her hair. He used to say: 'Fakhri, laugh so loud that I can't hear Fakhronissa coughing. Laugh loud . . .' Fakhri would cackle away. She used to say: 'Madame Fakhronissa, why are you so thin? Why don't you call Dr Abu Nuvas to examine you? Or at least cut down on the wine that you're drinking.' I said: 'What's the point. This consumption runs in the family: the Prince's grandfather and grandmother, his mother, too, but as for his paternal aunts . . . My father drank so much arak, smoked so much opium, he was just skin and bones. Not even forty years old and his hair was all white.'

She took another sip. The Prince sat there, with his head down.

'Prince, I don't know anything, but it looks as if you have nothing left.'

She drank again. Fakhronissa, she could be so cruel! She would say: 'Prince, I'll just sit here and wait until you are bankrupt and sell the house from under me.' The Prince said: 'I'll never touch your dowry or your jewels.' She replied: 'You won't have anything else. Just you wait.'

She raised the glass. I said: 'Prince, leave at least these bracelets and that necklace . . .'

He said: 'Alright, they are yours as well.'

The long-stemmed glass was now empty. Fakhronissa stood up. She had become as light as anything. Her white lace dress was loose on her, even at the shoulder. She said: 'Dear Prince, you really must get someone.'

The Prince said: 'I have a girl in mind. Her name is Fakhri. She's the daughter of the gardener I booted out. How would she be?'

She said: 'Fine. Just tell her to clear the table.'

The Prince said: 'Alright. You go to bed, Fakhronissa.'

Fakhronissa went to the door and said: 'Fakhri love, when you've finished, come up.'

She went into the hall and climbed the stairs. He was late again. Still, I'll wait up for him, however long he is. Why does he go and burn the books? Just when I was beginning to read out loud without a mistake. If he were out late I'd sit by the window and read:

The guards fall upon him, tear off his clothes, cut into him with pen knives and place candles in the wounds. Oboes are sounding. Crowds would have gathered and spat in his face. They light the candles. Two guards grip him under the arms and bring him forward. The people are clapping. From high up in the Governor's Palace, Grandfather observed the scene through field-glasses. The candles were burning and the people . . . The candle wax must have dripped on his skin. Who was he? The seminary students would certainly have spat at him and shouted: 'Damn your filth to Hell!'

She went into her bedroom. I know my way around here. I don't need a light.

She went and sat down on her bed, kicked off her shoes and crossed one foot over the other. Her feet were hot. I said: 'Fakhri love, is the Prince still not back?' She said: 'No.' I said: 'Then, telephone Dr Abu Nuvas that he should come.' She said: 'The Prince has cut off the phone.' He had also locked the door behind him. Why was he doing these things? He used to go off in the morning and come back at midnight. He used to go into my room, into Fakhri's room. He used to say: 'Laugh loud, Fakhri.' If I didn't laugh, he used to tickle me on the soles of my feet or under the armpit, or he hit me. He used to bury his head in my breasts and stop his ears with his two hands. Those days, Fakhri and I, or rather Fakhronissa and I, were all alone in that house from morning till night, two women all alone within those walls. Fakhronissa used to cast sidelong glances at me from behind her thick glasses. I used to say: 'Ma'am, it's not my fault.' She'd say: 'I know. You're a good girl.' Then she'd go back to coughing.

She stretched out on the bed. I wish I had lit the lamp. If the Prince comes, he lights it himself and says: 'Are you asleep, Fakhronissa?' I pretend to be asleep. He lies down beside me. Why does he always want to . . . He kisses even my fingers. That night what a scene he made about them! I said: 'What can I do? All on my own and . . .' He said: 'What have you to do with these things? I pay good money so that Fakhri does all the housework. All you have to do is sit and make yourself look pretty or read a book. Five years, morning till night, I've been trying to drum something into your head.' So, right in the middle of the night, I got up and had another wash. I have to put on scent, on my hair, my breast, my hands. But will the smell go away?

He sat in front of the stove and tossed the books into the flames. He was saying: 'Fakhronissa, stoke it well, so everything burns up. I don't want you, too, to . . .' I said: 'These are very valuable, Prince.' He said: 'Rake it over, Fakhronissa.' He held a photograph in front of my face, and said: 'Look! Great-grandfather!' Great-grandfather was kneeling, his two hands resting on his great thighs. He leaned against two or three cushions. Beneath him was a jewel-encrusted throne, or so the Prince said. His sword lay in his lap. He had a thick handlebar moustache. His eyes had vanished under his bushy eyebrows. He laughed. He laughed so loud I took fright. He shut the book and tossed it in the middle of the fire which flared up. I was hot. He had begun at sundown. He hadn't been drinking. All those books! And would they burn? For all that I stoked the fire. The flames jumped. My hands burned and my face was scorched. As for him, he sat in a chair, with the books piled up around him, one on top of the other, like roof tiles. One by one he'd pick them up and throw them into the fire. 'Stoke it up, Fakhronissa,' he'd be saying. Would it never end? Only the outsides of the books would burn. The inside stayed as white as they were. I went on stoking the flames. The pages turned red, curled over themselves, blackened, burst into flame. I was boiling hot. He kept on saying: 'Stoke it up, Fakhronissa.' Now it was Great-grandfather's *Memoirs*. The leather binding simply would not catch. The Prince said: 'No doubt he forgot to mention how he gave orders that all those men be encased alive in plaster. He certainly forgot to mention how he slit that boy's throat from ear to ear. Have you really never heard, Fakhronissa, why Grandfather killed his own mother, right there in His Grace's house?' What was he asking me for? Even Madame Fakhronissa did not know that. But she would say: 'Maybe, she slept with the gardener or . . .'

The mother takes her son's hand and leads him into the presence of Great-grandfather. She says: 'I don't know what's wrong, Excellency, this child just won't listen to me, he's always playing with his pigeons, runs away from school. Please consider commanding the chamberlains . . .' Great-grandfather cries out: 'Master Executioner!' (He held his photograph before my face. The man was very tall, with handlebar moustaches, with a long robe and boots. The Prince said: 'He always wore red,* but you can't see that in the photograph.' He stood with his arms crossed over his chest.) Master Executioner appears. He sits the boy on the ground. Great-grandfather says: 'Do you promise, boy, that you'll stop racing pigeons.' He starts to pace up and down, tapping the side of his boot with his whip. Master Executioner digs two fingers of his left hand into the boy's nostrils, pulls back his head and lays the blade of his dagger against his throat. The Prince continues to pace and shouts: 'Do you promise that you'll go to school, eh?' He taps his whip against his boot. Master Executioner puts his foot on the thigh of the kneeling boy. The boy tugs at Master Executioner's hand. He says not a word. His mouth was surely open. Else how could he have drawn breath? Maybe the air rattled in his throat or he whispered something nobody could hear. Great-grandfather says: 'Do you promise that from now on you'll do as your mother says?' And he taps the whip against his boot. The Prince did the same. The boy's mother, now she sees he can only croak, blurts out: 'I don't know, Your Something or Othership, pardon him. For the sake of Your Sereneneship, have mercy on him.'

* Nobody wore red in Qajar Iran, except the Executioners, known as the 'Lords of Wrath', and the villains of the Kerbela Passion Play.

Great-grandfather cries out: 'Master Executioner! Stay your hand!' Master Executioner slits the throat anyway, cuts off the head and tosses it at Great-grandfather's feet. 'You see,' said the Prince, 'no Master Executioner had ever heard the order, Stay your hand! . . . Stoke it up, Fakhronissa.' I stoked the fire. What a lot of books! I sat at the fire till dawn. He said: 'Fakhronissa, now for the panegyrics of Great-grandfather. Now for *Account of a Journey through Khorasan*.' He was tossing them in three at a time, shouting: 'Stoke her up, Fakhronissa.' There was so much ash collected in the stove!

The Prince still sat there, on the same chair, in the same room. He had the photographs framed and placed in the room. He said: 'Why didn't you stop me burning the photograph of Great-grandfather? He would have looked so well beside these ones.' I said: 'I had no idea.' He never leaves the house unlocked, with its high walls and the willow tree. If only he'd let somebody come in and change the water . . . The poor fish! He's always saying: 'You must not go into that room.' I say: 'But, Prince, haven't you seen how dusty the pictures are?'

He goes into that room every evening, all on his own, and how he coughs! She'd be bent over a book. I used to grip her shoulders. When the fit was over, she'd take my hands in her own little, white hands and say: 'You're a good girl, dear Fakhri.' And me carrying on like that, right before her eyes! Why did he behave like that? And Madame Fakhronissa right upstairs, in agonies ... and so pale, the colour of sour milk! He was always pouncing. He'd come into my bed. I'd say: 'Prince, it just isn't right that you . . .' and he'd say: 'What do you mean, It isn't right? My great-grandfather . . .' It was always Great-grandfather, he of that photograph, kneeling, with that bushy moustache, and that jewelled court robe and all those pearls stitched on the chest. Why did he encase people in plaster? Madame Fakhronissa used to read that sort of thing and daily got thinner and thinner. And then me and the Prince, right there in front of her, right in front of the corpse of my mistress. Not that it was my fault. He crept up on me. And I could never say No. He said: 'Come on, give us a good cackle, I want her to hear your voice.' How could I? With Madame Fakhronissa upstairs, stretched out on her bed, and blood . . . I said: 'Dear Prince, Madame passed away this afternoon.' Madame's eyes were quite blank. He picked me up. Where did he get the strength from? He carried me upstairs, all the way upstairs. He knocked on the door, saying: 'May I come in, please?' I said: 'Prince, I told you that her eyes were fixed on the ceiling.' Blood had dripped out of the corner of her mouth onto her beauty spot. And her eyes! The Prince laughed and said: 'All the better.' He opened the door and turned on the light. Madame Fakhronissa lay stretched out on the bed, her face drained of all colour. The blood had dried in the corner of her mouth. Beneath the dull lenses of her glasses, her eyes were still open, like two white china dishes. I said: 'Prince, it's over with her.' He said: 'Shut up, you!' The Prince pulled the bed sheet up over Fakhronissa's face. He lifted up her thin and weightless corpse and took it over to the wall and laid it on the floor. The sheet slipped down, and blood again ran onto Fakhronissa's cheek. The Prince took off her glasses and tossed them away. Those eyes! The blood was leaking through the sheet. I knelt down beside Madame. I didn't cry, just covered my face with my apron, so I didn't have to see Madame lying there, under that white sheet . . . The Prince grabbed my collar and ripped my dress at the back. I was kneeling down, above my mistress. I said: 'What are you trying to do, Prince?' He kicked me. I fell on my back on the floor. He tore off my apron and dress. My slip, as well. And his eyes! They were deep crimson, like two dishes of blood. He said: 'Hurry up! Get dressed!' He had in his hand Madame's lace wedding dress, and threw it over my naked body. I said: 'Prince, for God's sake, don't do this! Don't do this!' He took me by the arm and lifted me to my feet. He grabbed my arms and gave me a slap with his fingers. He unfastened my headscarf, took a handful of hair and said: 'Look there, Fakhronissa. Fakhri is dead. Dead.' He pulled my hair up at the back. Blood was still leaking out. I said: 'Have pity, Prince, with Madame . . .' He was holding the lace dress. It was Madame's dress. 'Sit down,' he said.

I sat down in front of the mirror. In the glass, it was still Fakhri, crying. Madame's make-up was on the dressing-table. In the mirror, I combed my hair. Then I tried to paint on the beauty spot. I had no control of myself. My hand was shaking. The Prince said: 'Put the beauty spot at the left-hand corner of your mouth, Fakhronissa.' I wasn't in control of myself. He painted the beauty spot himself. The Prince's hands were steady. He looked at me from out of the mirror, smiling. With his thumb he wiped away my tears. It wasn't Madame in the mirror. It was Fakhri. She wasn't crying. If only I could have coughed, like my mistress.

He hugged me and took me to bed. He undressed and lay down beside me. He was laughing and running his hand all over my body and my legs. He buried his head in my hair. I twisted my head round. There lay Madame, stretched out under the white sheet soaked in blood. Her glasses lay on the carpet in the corner. Her books were all over the shelves, on the mantelpiece and on the table. The Prince turned my face to his, began to tickle me, said: 'Laugh, Fakhronissa. Laugh.' I looked at Madame and the blood leaking out again through the sheet. Madame's corpse was long and thin. The Prince slapped me on the face, and cried: 'Fakhronissa my darling, you were never like this!' I said: 'I am not Fakhronissa.' He wanted to do it, but I couldn't. I couldn't stop staring at Madame and her spectacles lying on a corner of the carpet medallion. He said: 'Why aren't you cackling, Fakhronissa?' He laid his hand on my arm and looked at me. He supported himself on his left arm, with his back to Madame. I couldn't see Madame's spectacles any more. He said: 'Are you afraid, Fakhronissa?' He wiped away my tears, and drew his fingers over my face, my lips, my nose. Again he dried my tears and said: 'You're frightened, aren't you?' I could only stare at the ceiling and the floral patterns of the stucco work and the cherub in the petunia flower . . . The Prince said: 'If only somebody had turned the light out! You aren't afraid, Fakhronissa?' He closed my eyelids. If only I could have coughed like Madame. If only I were asleep. If only I were dead.

Prince Ehtejab had his head bowed, resting on both

hands. Fakhronissa sat over on her swivel chair, holding an album. The carnation was still in the flower vase. Grandfather was still seated in his chair. The Prince coughed. The windows rattled.

She said: 'Look, Prince, there I am!' She was sucking her thumb. She was being held by Grandmama, who had a hand on her thigh. Grandmama was sitting on a stool, with her head held quite straight. The photographer gentleman must have said, 'Look this way, please, Grandmama, this way', and taken the photograph. She had her left arm round Fakhronissa. To the left of them was a vase with long-stemmed flowers. Beyond the flowers you could see only the tall, white jets of the fountain.

'Fakhronissa,' I said, 'did Grandmama always have white hair?'

She said: 'As far as I remember, always.'

She just sucked her thumb. Little Aunt used to send Nanny Ghamar over to her first husband, Mutamid Mirza, with the message: 'Let them take the child away with them. I want to raise her myself.' The baby would have been asleep in her cradle, her thumb in her mouth. Nanny Ghamar said: 'How pretty she is, Grandma'am! Lord above, wouldn't it be a shame for such a pretty child to grow up without a mother?' Grandmama said:

'Nayereh Khatun should have thought of that earlier, not now, when it's too late.' Nanny Ghamar said: 'It wasn't Madame's fault. His Highness ordered her to ask for a divorce and she obeyed.'

Mutamid Mirza refused. As he comes out of the Governor's Palace – he was in a carriage – and drives down to the river, he sees that a crowd has gathered. He has with him an official escort of guards and footmen, and tells them, 'See what the matter is.' The guards charge in among the people and drive them back with batons. A donkey lay half-dead on the river bank. The people were drinking its blood. Was the famine so bad that men were drinking donkey's blood . . .? But of course: Grandfather and the mullahs had cornered all the wheat and were hoarding it in their own warehouses. When it spoiled, they tipped it at night into the river. In addition, there had been no rain. The river would have dried to a trickle. Mutamid Mirza returns to the Governor's Palace. He hands the Prince's Robe of Honour and pen-case to the secretaries to deliver to the Prince then goes to his own house and shuts the door. Whoever Grandfather sends, Mutamid Mirza says the same thing: 'I will be no man's servant again.'

His two children were dead, one in the cholera year, one stillborn. Grandfather sends a message commanding him to divorce the Lady Nayereh Khatun or face the consequences. Mutamid Mirza writes in Arabic in the margin of the letter: 'As thy highest will commands, so it shall be obeyed.' He also wrote: 'All that this slave possesses was acquired in the service of Your Highness and pertains to the Slaves of the Threshold of the Most Serene and Illustrious Seat of Justice.' He added: 'Whenever you command, it will be surrendered to you. In the matter, however, of my honoured consort, the Lady Nayereh Khatun, this will be submitted to the rulings of the highest spiritual authorities in conformity with the most enlightened religious practice.' The guards are despatched and, in conformity with their orders, bastinado Mutamid Mirza and take Nayereh Khatun away. She may have been pregnant, I don't know and nor did Fakhronissa, but she did say: 'Perhaps she was.' Later on they send Fakhronissa to Mutamid Mirza's house. They make Little Aunt go through a formal ceremony of divorce in the presence of the Imam of the Congregational Mosque.* The plan was to betroth Nayereh Khatun to the son of the Prime Minister so as to strengthen Grandfather's position. But the Minister falls out of favour and Grandfather abandons the scheme.

* The leading clergyman in Isfahan.

Nanny Ghamar says: 'Grandma'am, do let me take the child with me. Nayereh Khatun misses the child terribly, and anyway a child needs its mother.' Grandmama replies: 'So what's Mother got that I haven't, eh?' Nanny Ghamar said . . . I don't know, she must have said something because Grandmama put her hand in the pocket of her dress and pulled out this big kerchief. It was knotted to make dummies or comforters. Fakhronissa said: 'Grandmama picks up a big Yazdi silk kerchief, heaps sugar on the corners and sides and ties them round with string, says: Look at all these, just as good as the breast, with these I can bring up my child.'

Grandfather sends the guards. They bring Mutamid Mirza to the citadel and throw him in the dungeon. But for all that they search the house they can find neither Fakhronissa nor Grandmama. They plunder anything of value and put a seal on the house. Grandfather is in no doubt at all that Grandmama will try and take her case to the capital. He puts men on the city gates. But Grandmama gets to the capital across the desert with just one servant and a hired donkey. She rides the donkey, with Fakhronissa in her arms. The servant leads the donkey by the bridle. Grandmama goes to the house of one of the royal ladies, Madame Anis or somebody else, and requests asylum. Madame Anis intercedes for her to the effect that Grandfather will leave Mutamid Mirza alone. By now, he'd have been just skin and bone. His hands and legs had been scarred by the stocks and chains. He'd written a deed of assignment, stating: 'The entirety of my real property and estates and my deposited specie of my own free will and voluntarily I surrender to His Most Magnificent and Glorious Highness.' Grandfather does not return the estates, with the exception of the house. Mutamid Mirza was also provided with a pension, but that was from Great-grandfather.

Little Aunt was then betrothed to the Imam of the Congregational Mosque. I remember it well. Within two years she was back at home. Every now and then she used to go with her servants to see Fakhronissa. Fakhronissa could remember only two dark eyes visible though a slit in the door. She used just to look and go away. Fakhronissa said: 'Grandmama used to say, "If you go to the door, they'll take you off and burn you with hot irons, just like your Daddy. Look how they branded him."' They had burned the backs of Mutamid Mirza's hands because Grandfather wanted to know where he had put the rest of his money. Mutamid Mirza used to sit at his opium brazier, once in the morning, once in the evening. In all this time what would Fakhronissa have been up to?

With that old white-haired Grandmama who holds her neck so straight in the photograph. They had flowers. You can see that from the vase in the photograph. There was also a pool. Fakhronissa would have played in the garden, among the flowers, talking to them. She would have picked a carnation and put it in the corner of her mouth. Grandmama, of course, would have been sitting up on the terrace and, taking up her knitting, would have said: 'Now don't be going to the door, girl!'

Fakhronissa would also have gone to the pool, to be by the fish. Her father was always crying out. She herself said: 'From morning to night he lay on his right side and Grandmother blew on the embers for him.' Fakhronissa would surely have sat by the brazier, on the other side from her father. She'd have sat there in the evenings. Mornings and afternoons she was at school. Grandmama took Fakhronissa to school and brought her back. (Grandfather had fallen from grace, else he would have tried to snatch Fakhronissa.) So there they would have been, Fakhronissa and Grandmama and her crippled father with all those books, one little garden, one pool, and one door with Little Aunt peering through a slit in it. When not groaning or dozing, Mutamid Mirza used to say: 'Read out loud, my darling.' Fakhronissa had long hair and her cheeks . . . Her cheeks? I don't know.

Perhaps they'd have been white as they were at the end
. . . white or red . . . white or red? The photograph was
black-and-white. Mutamid Mirza's moustache would
have been ash-grey, his hair thin . . . and the nose? He
would have supported himself on a cushion and smoked
his opium and said: 'Read, my darling.'

His pension would not have gone far. Grandmama
had a lot of jewellery, but sold it off piece by piece. The
books they also sold, even the best antiques. Of
Grandmama's jewels a few pieces survived and passed
down to Fakhronissa. One morning they see that
Mutamid Mirza is dead. He was lying dead in his bed,
with his mouth open and white foam round his lips, his
eyes open and fixed on the ceiling. Fakhronissa was ten,
she said so herself. No doubt she would have been slim
with those same two soft dimples each side of her mouth
and the beauty spot just on the left. Her dress . . . what
sort of dress was it? White? Probably. And those
spectacles. No, she would have worn those only later.
Haidar Ali, their servant, said to Fakhronissa: 'This is
the doing of Dr Abu Nuvas.' Nobody knows, but
Grandfather made a habit of that sort of thing.
Especially as Mutamid Mirza had nothing more for
Grandfather to get his hands on. Grandmama stays on
with her servant and his wife and Fakhri. Fakhri would

still have been little, pink and white. Little Aunt would certainly have sent somebody to fetch her daughter. But Grandmama would not give her up. Fakhri said: 'Grandmama could no longer walk. She used to drag herself along the ground to the terrace, or sat on the steps with her eyes fixed on the street door.'

Lunchtime or afternoon, when Fakhronissa came back from school . . . Fakhronissa wore a pinafore. With her school bag in her hand, she'd have opened the door and seen Grandmama sitting on the steps, the other side of the fountain. Would there have been a flower vase beside her? She'd have run, run all the way down the boulevard. The wind would have played with her hair and the hem of her pinafore. She'd have swung her school bag. Grandmama would have opened her arms and watched her granddaughter running towards her on her little legs. She'd have seen how her hair had . . . but then she'd have hugged her, and planted a kiss on her beauty spot, and with an unsteady, old finger pushed back a couple of strands of hair that had strayed over her granddaughter's forehead. It would have been like that, perhaps.

As for Grandmama, what would she have been thinking? Maybe she would have wanted to go on living and dragging herself from her room to the hall and from there to the terrace and from there to the top of the steps, there to sit and wait. One day, of course, she can't go on. They'll support her under the arms, Fakhri and her mother. No, Fakhri was still too little, she wouldn't have been able to manage. Fakhri's mother and Haidar Ali take her under the arms. And then . . . what then? Why didn't I ask Fakhronissa? Now and then, Little Aunt meets her on the way to or from school and takes her into her carriage. Fakhronissa said: 'At first, I was frightened they'd take me off and burn me with hot irons.' She sits Fakhronissa down opposite her and looks her up and down. Fakhronissa would surely have wanted to look out of the carriage window. (I scratched her eyes out, and it was the right thing to do.)

Fakhronissa, who also did not care for her, said: 'She'd start off just sitting and staring at me, and then she'd say: "You're my daughter, you know, and that opium addict of a father of yours was not worthy of me. You shouldn't be frightened of me."'

She would surely have been sitting bolt upright. Fakhronissa would frown. She would wag her finger and say: 'You're my daughter, you should be proud of me. For two whole years, I was the wife of the Imam of the Congregational Mosque, the wife of Sayyid Hassan the Jurisprudent, don't you know?' Then she'd burst out laughing. Alright, but afterwards . . . what about afterwards? When Grandmama could no longer sit even on the terrace, at the top of the steps . . .?

Fountain. Flower vase. Grandmama with her white hair and Fakhronissa sucking her thumb. And the photographer gentleman. And then . . .? Then Grandmama dies, at her prayers or in bed or on the terrace. It makes no difference, she is dead. That leaves Fakhronissa, that huge house, Fakhri, Haidar Ali and Fakhri's mother. Now Fakhri's mother dies. Dies in childbirth. Haidar Ali then married a woman in my own household. What a pest he was! He came along and said: 'My daughter and I go together. Anybody interested in my daughter will have to put up with me.' I threw him out. It just wouldn't work. If I'd given in, every time Fakhri caught sight of her little father with his round white beard and old hands, she'd have been reminded she was Fakhri, not Fakhronissa. I did the right thing. He lived for two more years. I continued to pay him. He said: 'If you don't marry Fakhri, I'll bring an action in court.' I said: 'Do your worst, I don't care.' I gave him his wages. Promptly every month I sent him his pension. I rented two rooms for him. He used to sit on the edge of the terrace and smoke his pipe. Why do old people always sit on the edge of the terrace, or on the side of the pool?

Little Aunt married again, but much later, after Grandfather died. She had no more children. Vase. Fountain. Grandmama, who was now dead . . . How good it would have been if I had had other photographs of Fakhronissa! I would have hung them all in this room.

She stood beside the little canal. She was tall and slender in her black dress. Her arms were bare and pure white. She had tossed her braids back. She had her spectacles on. Her dress had delicate pleats around the waist. The hem was a band of pleated white lace. Her legs were slim and white in their dark ankle boots. She stood there, in profile, nose, one eye, sculpted neck. I held the horse by the bridle. Murad was there, or maybe not. Fakhronissa *was* there. I looked at her. She looked at me through the glass of those spectacles of hers. Her eyes were still dark and lively. She turned her head. Was Murad there? He must have been, because I climbed into the saddle, and Murad helped me up. I galloped off, wheeled about, came back, galloped off again, wheeled about. She wasn't watching. I dismounted and handed Murad the reins. I came back through the trees, in shadow except where a few splashes of light fell on the leaves and branches. Songbirds twittered. I broke off a branch. There she was, at the end of the long green arcade, in the blinding glare of the sunshine. I had the branch in my hand. She was standing and looking at me, and smiling that bitter smile that made one long to hide one's face or stand before a full-length mirror and examine oneself minutely. I turned about. The branch in my hand was quite bare: I'd stripped off all the leaves. I broke off another, came out from among the trees to the edge of the basin, beneath those stone maidens with the water pouring from their mouths. They were stark naked, with little breasts and plump bellies. I looked down into the water. My hair was untidy. I turned about. She was still standing, over there beyond the trees, on the gravel walk. I smoothed down my hair and turned onto the path. I walked past her, on the other side of the path, beside the little channel. I kept my eyes on the water and the leaves floating down in the water, when suddenly she said: 'Khosrow Khan, it can't be that you're in love, can it?' I turned about and there she was, with that smile and those eyes and the two dimples each side of the mouth.

If only I'd begun here, and not with that faded photograph of Grandmama and the fountain and the flower vase. Well, it's all gone now. I do know that I said nothing. She came forward. She herself came forward and put her hand under my chin. I lifted my head. That smile of hers! If only I could somehow have wiped away that smile. Fakhri can't do it, could never ever smile like that. I did my best, but she couldn't do it. She'd open her mouth and show her coarse teeth and laugh, out loud, the imbecile! But Fakhronissa . . . It was as if in the conjunction of those dimples at the corners of her mouth, and those eyes and even the round O of her lips, there was something that scared one to death. One felt how small and insignificant one was, even if one was the grandson of His Highness. I wished I were dead.

Prince Ehtejab coughed. He coughed long and loud and his shoulders shook.

Her hands were slim and white. Her black dress showed off her figure. She said: 'Khosrow Khan, are you blushing? That is extraordinary. Here with so many ladies in the household! And you, with such a fine figure and address! Surely, you . . .'

How did she know? With Munireh Khatun I just . . .

Grandfather said: 'Playing, were you?' He knelt on his throne. I stared at the hairs on his chest. He had his doublet on. Mother held my hand. Mother's hand was shaking. Grandfather said: 'Let go of his hand. He's no child, it seems.' Grandmother said: 'It's not the child's fault.' Grandfather asked in a quiet voice: 'Who else have you been playing with, Khosrow Khan? Who else apart from Munireh Khatun have you been playing bareback horsey with, eh?' I said: 'With . . .' I was about to say, Nusratosadat . . . He hit me. Grandfather struck me with his stick across the ankle. And O, how Munireh Khatun screamed and screamed!

Munireh Khatun was standing in the private quarters beside a small basin. Her hair was cut short, like a boy's. She had on a long, flowery dress. She shook the water in the basin. She was rail-thin. I could see the nape of her neck, which was white and covered in fine down. I went up to the basin. She did not look at me or speak. She just bent over the basin and shook the water. The water welled up and Munireh Khatun's image trembled. Her hair spread and rippled. I stood on tip-toe. The water subsided. Why was she always standing at the basin, agitating the water? She bent over the water and stared into it. She had reddened her lips. With what? I don't know. Even her chin was rouged. It surely wasn't lipstick. She'd lost two of her front teeth. I said: 'What are you hoping to see, Munireh Khatun?' She said: 'So you've turned up again, turned up again, Khosrow Khan?' She went on saying that and gazing into the water, then shaking it and peering into the ripples. What was she searching for? I took hold of the basin and looked in. The water was crystal clear. There were no fish in it, just the image on the surface of the water pipe standing on the other side of the basin. She said: 'Did you see it, Khosrow Khan?' I said: 'See what? See what?' She said: 'When the water moves, you watch.' She shook the water. I looked but saw nothing, except Munireh Khatun's face, elongated at first, welling up, then breaking into countless pieces. Then it was Munireh Khatun's face again with that short hair and those red lips. I said: 'It's just your reflection.' She said: 'You cannot see it. Nor can His Highness. I'm the only one who can, I'm the only one.'

Laleh Aga said: 'She's mad. Keep away from her.' I said: 'I really want to see.' He said: 'See what?' I said: 'Munireh Khatun obviously can see something in the water of the basin, and that's why she's always bent over and staring into it.' He said: 'She's mad, Khosrow Khan. I said she was mad.' I said: 'Munireh Khatun, would you like to play with me, play horsey? I'd really like to.' She cried out: 'I saw it. I saw it.' She was stooped over the rippling water. I said: 'What did you see?' She only stared into the ripples. What was she seeing? How did I get onto Munireh Khatun?

Fakhronissa . . . If only I had a photograph. Vase . . . Carnation . . .

Fakhronissa took me by the hand. How light her hand was! We walked under the trees through that long green arcade that led into shadow and, beyond the trees, the deep well and that column of plaster. She stooped, picked up a couple of stones, and put them in the palm of my hand. She looked at me, laughing. That smile of hers. In the glare of the sun there was no place to hide. She said: 'Fire away!' I said: 'At what?' She said: 'Your head really is in the clouds, Prince. Your great-grandfather was only satisfied if every morning he could trample on the bones of his blood enemies, the magnificent remains* of Nader[†] and the Zands, and you are too timid to toss a stone at a fellow who has been encased in plaster for at least twenty years. Courage, Prince! Hurry up and gladden your old grandfather's soul. After all this snake of a servant was an informer for the Prime Minister of the time. My father told me. Believe me. When Grandfather found out, he gave orders that he be encased alive in plaster up here, on this little knoll, so

* 'Who can revive these magnificent [bones] now they are decomposed?' Koran, 36:78.
[†] After the collapse of the Safavid Empire, Nader Quli Khan seized power, was crowned Shah in 1736, invaded India and brought back the Peacock Throne from Delhi. Assassinated in 1747, he was succeeded by the Zand dynasty which ruled from Shiraz. The Zands were themselves displaced in the 1780s by the Qajars, of whom Prince Ehtejab is the fictional heir.

that he should have a clear view of everything and report it to his master.'

I had the stones in my hand and there, on a stone base at the top of a short flight of steps, could just be made out the silhouette in plaster of a man. How was it that I had never noticed? I said: 'I never knew it. Laleh Aga never told me.' She said: 'Now you do know, what are you standing around for? Quick, stone him to death!'

Who was this spy? What was his name? Fakhronissa didn't know either. She said: 'One out of fifteen millions. What's the difference? Just a man, that's all.' I myself gave the order to pull it down. I didn't go myself. I told them to bury him where he was. There were others in the wall of the deep well and even in . . . It was filled in. Why did they do these things? Father was a good man, Murad used to say. Murad knew Father well. Fakhronissa said: 'He killed a lot of men, but the good thing about Father was that he did not watch, it did not happen before his eyes, it wasn't an everyday thing, just one hour and bang! All done! In one go, between two and five hundred wounded and dead.'

Fakhronissa said: 'Alright, let's go. There's not a single drop of your great ancestors' blood in your veins.' I threw the stones away.

Father was sitting in the middle saloon, leaning

against a cushion. He had another cushion under his
legs, and a lit brazier in front of him. There were
cushions to his left and right. Mirza Nasrullah was
blowing on the coals for him. Father said: 'How quickly
you've got to know each other!' Father's moustache was
ash-grey. He blew the smoke out through his nose and
his mouth. Fakhronissa said nothing. She had let go of
my hand. We had been walking through the rooms when
we came on him. Father said: 'Good. Go now and get to
know each other better.'

Fakhronissa said: 'Nayereh Khatun must have written
that we two should be married.' She told me that later.
She never referred to her as Mother. She used to sit on
the balcony and read. When I came up to her, beside the
balcony balustrade, she said: 'Prince, don't hang about
with nothing to do. Idleness isn't good for you. You
should have something to do.' I went hunting by jeep. It
was not pleasant. We pursued the gazelles so hard they
collapsed. Their tongues hung from their mouths. How
red they were! Their stomachs palpitated. And those
little hooves and sweet, black eyes and that shocked and
fearful look. Only cards were fun. Full house, kings on
queens. When I saw the other player's hand tremble, or
saw him lower his eyes or stub his cigarette out in the
ash-tray . . . it was for those things that I took him on. I

had to find some way to squander all my property and estates. When I had nothing in my hand, I bluffed.

Fakhronissa used to say: 'That is not doing something. You are fooling yourself. You must do something that is really something, that will at least get you into the history books. Get your gun and go to the garden fence and, anybody passing on the other side, take aim and fire. Then stand there and watch the victim bleed to death. But if you take a dislike to somebody, if the fellow is misquoting a couplet of verse or blowing his nose in public or putting a foot on your doorstep to tie up his shoe, then you are not authorised to take a shot at him. The more groundless the quarrel, the better. The person who is always looking for justification for killing somebody is not only a murderer but a liar, and a liar who is trying to fool himself to boot. If you want to kill somebody, you don't need a justification. You just take aim at his head, or his chest, and pull the trigger, like so. Look, learn from your illustrious ancestors. Out hunting if they found no game, they'd shoot at human beings, children even. They'd stand round and look over the quivering heap of arms and legs and staring eyes.'

She laughed noiselessly, with those dimples of hers beside the mouth and those unblinking eyes behind the spectacle glasses. I couldn't bear to be at home. I'd come back, dead drunk, at midnight so at least the lines by her mouth were all smoothed away and the spectacles off and the eyelids shut. She'd be lying stretched on the bed in her white shift, her hair spread across the pillow. She'd say: 'Put the light out, Prince.'

Prince Ehtejab said aloud: 'It was just like that . . . and . . . and . . .'

And he coughed.

What was going behind that smooth forehead? How could one look out from those eyes, and from behind those thick lenses take in me and Fakhri and all the old furniture and things and the lines of print in books and the mirror that reveals that every day the two delicate lines on the forehead were getting deeper?

If I, like my noble ancestors, could have sat on a jewel-inlaid throne beneath a climbing rose and given orders that the attendants, that the Executioner bring in the prisoner for sentencing . . . The condemned man should have his hands tied behind his back. One night, or one week, one month, with a block on his feet and his hands in chains, he must be confined in prison. Light? No doubt the light through the well in the vault will be adequate. What use are those pallid beams in a dank prison? Perhaps only the dust can show the passage of light through the blackness of the dungeon. There should be whipping. If we ourselves can be present, better still. With a glance at us, the guards strike harder. A bag of gold coins should be tossed their way. The louder the shrieks, the harder they strike and the harder they strike, naturally, the louder the shrieks. Underneath the rambling rose, in the cool shade, the air filled with scent. On his face there should not be a scratch. We have expressly prohibited that there should . . . After all, the head must be sent as a tribute to the county town or the capital of the Guarded Realms* and the reward collected. They roll out the execution mat. The Executioner, will he be dressed in red? Naturally. His moustachios must reach to his ears. The gleam of the dagger. The dagger beneath the Executioner's sash. And we, since we have given orders that the oven be lit at sundown, know full well that, look!, a heap of glowing coals has been building under a layer of ash. The Executioner glances towards us. We nod our hallowed head. The Executioner has inserted two fingers into the condemned man's nose. Which condemned man? Whoever he may be, he's a fellow whose head is worth something. Behind the lines of his forehead are thoughts of which we have no knowledge. What we do know is that he is a menace,

* Iran.

who . . . The Executioner places the dagger to the prisoner's throat. While we sit there, waiting for the blood to spout, we take a stem of briar rose between our teeth. The blood begins to gush. The prisoner is palpitating. (Or isn't? I never witnessed such a thing. Grandfather and Great-grandfather saw it often.) And then . . . then the Executioner is holding the prisoner's bloody scalp in his hand. I see the staring eyes of the prisoner. Even when it sickens me, so as to uphold the might of my prestige, I may not take my eyes off the blood and head and the headless trunk, bound at the hands and quivering on the ground, and the guards and the Executioner and the head on its spit, which he holds in the oven, in the midst of the brightest flames, so it should be easier for him to skin.

The head must be skinned, otherwise it will stink, especially as the roads are long and lawless. Once the head is stuffed with straw and brought into our hallowed presence, how could one ever understand what had gone on behind that brow and those big, empty eye-sockets and that toothless mouth? Maybe that's the reason the noble forefathers first threw the prisoner into the dungeon. Maybe, too, because they could not look in on the prisoner through a window or a crack in the door, they would assign him an informer to note his every movement and every word and submit a report each evening. The guards would open the door, and bring in a chair or a fleece for him to sit on. The informer would observe and take notes. But what if the dirty wretch of a prisoner would not even groan, or worse, fell asleep, what then? Then they'd wake him up with a few kicks. There'd be a bowl of water by him and a crust of bread.

If the convicted man grasps that there in the darkness, there is somebody sitting on a chair or on a fleece and observing him and writing it all down, he'll certainly withdraw into his skin – a skin which can be easily removed and filled up with straw – or maybe he won't: either he sings his heart out or must needs have his tongue loosened with a pen-knife. If the convicted man is frightened, if he begs and whines, should one not find him a soulmate? After all, there's no shortage. One who like him has had a taste of the whip, the block on his feet and the chain round his neck, there, beside him, stretched out, whimpering . . . And then again if the prisoner keeps silent, if he's always thinking, trying to guess what's going on under the skin of the new arrival, if he wants to put himself behind those eyes . . . ? Finally, if the prisoner does fall to talking and it all spills out, how is the informer going to commit it all to memory or to paper and submit a report? Which gesture and which sentence will he remember, and which forget? In the accumulation of these disconnected and broken sentences and of those gestures that have meaning only at the instant of their occurrence, how can one penetrate the depths of flesh and skin and arteries and nerves that constitute a human being? Or make it anew from scratch? Why shouldn't both prisoner and informer be freed? Two persons at liberty within high walls who pass the time with a garden plot and a little pool and a willow tree and a few hundred books? And as for me? I . . .

Prince Ehtejab felt the immense weight of his head in his shuddering hands.

The walls were high. I had to search hard to find this house. Four rooms were enough for two human beings to rattle around in. Fakhri said: 'Prince, Madame was coughing today. So badly, I was frightened.'

I said: 'Did she cough up blood, eh?'

She said: 'No, Prince. God forbid! Her mouth was just a little bit red at the side. Madame quickly wiped it away with a handkerchief. I said: "I'm worried about you, Madame. Do you want Doctor . . .?" She said: "No, there's nothing to worry about."'

I said: 'Then . . . What did she do then, Fakhri?'

She said: 'Madame said: "Don't say a word to the Prince." I said: "No, Ma'am."'

Fakhri reeked of cob and soapy water – hands, apron, hair. She said: 'Madame stood up and went over to the pool. Her face was drained of colour. She said: "Fakhri, put the chair by the pool." I put it there. She said: "Fakhri, this house is so depressing, with all these rooms." (It was a house for all seasons, the family house.) I said: "Why's that, Madame." She said: "I don't know, but I absolutely refuse to die here. If only the Prince had found another house. This building is getting shabby. And you can't manage all these rooms all on your own. If only the Prince had sold the place."'

Fakhri's body was warm and naked and coursing with blood. T.B. wouldn't begin to breach those living defences. I said: 'What then?'

She said: 'She sat by the pool, and said: "Fakhri, take off my stockings." I said: "At your service, Ma'am." I took off her stockings.'

I said: 'What were her feet like, Fakhri? Did you like them?'

She said: 'They were white as anything, Prince.'

Fakhronissa steps on the lip of the pool – the lip was cold – and then on the next step down among all those fish. The fish swim up and nibble at Fakhronissa's toes. Fakhronissa had a high fever. She had difficulty breathing. I said:

'Had she put on her spectacles, Fakhri?'

She said: 'Yes, Prince. She even said: "Fakhri love, would you kindly go and bring me the book lying on the table."'

I said: 'She sat by the pool and read her book?'

She said: 'I brought the book and saw Madame had her hands on her knees and was gazing at something. I said: "Madame, here you are." She said nothing, just went on gazing. I said: "Madame, I brought your book." Madame started. She shuddered. She turned, took off her glasses and said: "Is that you, Fakhri?" I said: "Ma'am, your book." She said: "Oh yes, give it to me."'

I said: 'What happened then?'

She said: 'Nothing happened then. She put the book in her lap and went back to gazing.'

I said: 'At what?'

She said: 'That's what I don't know. In front of her were those stone girls that pour water out of their mouths, and the fountain, and the avenue. There were plane trees as well. A carrion crow was perched in the middle of the avenue, picking at a bone.'

I said: 'Didn't she gaze at the sky?'

She said: 'I don't know, Prince. I didn't go round to see Madame from the front. I thought she certainly would not like it if I did.'

I gave a slap. I slapped Fakhri on the face. I said: 'Haven't I told you . . .?'

She started crying.

I said: 'Then what?'

I had wiped away her tears. She couldn't speak for sobbing. She said at last: 'I went to the kitchen to see about dinner. When I came back, I said: "Madame, would you like me to light the lamps?" You see dusk was coming on. She said: "No, Fakhri, just put that fur coat over my shoulders."'

I said: 'Was she still looking straight ahead?'

She said: 'Absolutely, Prince. But her feet were no longer in the water.'

I said: 'Was the crow there?'

She said: 'No, it wasn't.'

I said: 'Was the patch of sky there still visible?'

She said: 'I didn't look. I think it wasn't.'

I said: 'Down there, at the bottom of the garden, could you see the door?'

She said: 'I think so.'

I said: 'What did Fakhronissa say?'

She said: 'Madame just said: "You're a good girl, Fakhri."'

Carrion crow. Bone. Stone maidens. Fountain. Ripples in the water ... The crow first pecks at the bone, then picks it up in its beak, or leaves it, and flies off over the trees or through the trees. Was Fakhronissa watching? If she saw it, would all her senses have been fixed on that crow and that bone and those wings and the flight amid the ... the ... ?

As long as it is light you can see the door. Little Aunt had been dead for years. Those eyes of hers ... Even if a passerby peeped through a crack in the door, it was too far to see anything. But Fakhronissa could see, even if no-one was peeping. She could see those anxious, dark eyes and their owner, that is, Little Aunt, chadored and veiled to the nines, standing the other side of the door and with a mixture of fear and pride, affection and disgust and ... I don't know what she was waiting for unless it was maybe that the slim little girl should appear again alone on the terrace, or in the cool shade of the trees or beside the pool.

It was sunny and that patch of sky could be seen through the tops of the trees. If there had been a scrap of cloud in the sky, then maybe a few drops of rain would have fallen in the pool. Fakhri said that or maybe she didn't. All she used to say was: 'I don't know, I don't know.' Imbecile! Fakhronissa with her slim body and the soft breeze that was blowing . . . ?

They used to give the prisoners water, just a few swallows a day. So that they wouldn't need to be taken out all the time and at least the dungeon wouldn't start to stink. Just a single piece of bread. They'd thrown him into one of the rooms in the public part of the house until he confessed what else he had and where he had hidden it. Suddenly he sees the Executioner, with his vast frame filling the doorway, dagger in his hand. The point of the dagger was dripping blood. The Executioner stood there and stared. Every now and then, maybe, he'd have stroked the dagger's sharp blade and eyed Mutamid Mirza. Mutamid Mirza looks down at the rosettes of the carpet and traces with his finger the entire outline of one of the arabesques, says: 'So, what are you waiting for? Come on, get on with it!' The Executioner says: 'His Highness ordered me to take the fee for executing Aga Habib from Mutamid.' Fakhronissa used to tell that story. Had she read it somewhere or her father told her? It makes no difference.

Would Fakhronissa have thought about all these things? Or about . . . about the crow and that path and the shade of the trees? Or about the branches that met at the end of the path and formed that vault, that green vault? Or the incessant, monotonous splash of the fountain? How far can sparrows fly when their eyes have been gouged with a pen-knife? He put up a ladder, climbed up and pulled a couple of sparrows from under the false arch. They must have been fledged because otherwise they couldn't have flown. How far? Did he gouge out the eyes up there on the ladder, or down below? Anyway, he gouged them out. Is that the sort of thing you inherit or not? Is it in the blood? I who could not bear to go on hunting. Just seeing a wild duck covered in blood . . . or hanging from the mouth of a saluki upsets me. How could a child of thirteen, even one just appointed Provincial Governor, have done such things? What was his tutor fellow doing . . .? Gouged out the eyes of sparrows, one by one, then let them go to fly. How far? Would they have crashed into the trees or a wall? Would he be laughing? I don't know. Maybe he would just have watched to see if this time one would . . . or bet that this one would make it to the pine tree or, when he saw it didn't, another one. And why? Who would want to read about these things?

Fakhri said: 'She just sat there and stared.' The crow had flown off. The sun was setting. If Fakhronissa had turned her head she'd have seen the pink of dusk. But she didn't turn her head, or maybe she did turn and see and remark it. Or she didn't and then . . . when it was dark, what then? Without doubt, lamplight shone out from the house, maybe from the window on the west side or . . . and the splash of the fountains and the chirping crickets, then as right now, like an endless thread of sound . . . When one stares into darkness, over there, one knows what can happen, not what is happening. That's why the darkness has much to tell. When I used to come home late, I'd know she was sitting by the window, in the darkness . . . staring into the darkness . . . or maybe the whole time did Fakhronissa have her eyes closed, or had fallen asleep . . . and was dreaming?

In the house I inherited from my family she had something to occupy her every moment, thinking about all those wriggling ladies in Grandfather's harem and the clergy . . . This house I bought. I liked the look of the outside walls. I thought, It'll be a good to cut down the willow tree, pave over the little garden and even fill in the pool. But it wasn't to be. If she had found out, it just could not be. I said to myself, Alright, it doesn't matter. Haidar Ali was also with me. I'd found him another wife. I told them to set up in the corner, in the room by the gate and not to stir from there except to tend to the garden and do the shopping. But when I saw they were breeding away – two in under two years – I threw them out. I did the right thing. He went to his paternal cousin. After Fakhronissa passed away, he showed up again. 'Take Fakhri, take me.' Idiot!

At the beginning, I didn't lock the gate. I had them bring fruit and vegetables to the house. The tenants brought them in or they came from the bazaar, so nobody had to go out. Only now and then, when Fakhronissa insisted, we went to the country. Doctor's orders . . . also Doctor's orders that she should not drink. I had charged the tenants to make wine each year and bring it in. There were always a few demijohns in the cellar. She drank after midday and then again at dinner. And in the mornings? Fakhri would say: 'Now and then, but only one glass, and that was it.' Fakhri used to say: 'In the mornings, Madame walks all the time in the court-yard.' If I got up early, I used to see her from the balcony. She'd be walking with her spectacles in her hand. Under her long white lace dress you could see her figure. The nape of her neck was white as snow. Her hair fell down over her breast. As she walked she chewed on a green stem. At times when she was overcome by coughing she went and sat down on her chair under the willow tree.

She was seated on her chair. She had her spectacles on. Toying with her hair, she said:

'You're waiting, Prince, are you?'

I said: 'Fakhronissa, so early in the morning you'll catch cold, especially in this lace dress.'

She said: 'Early or late, what difference does it make? How much did you lose last night, Prince?'

I said: 'Nothing to boast about.'

She said: 'Don't you catch cold.'

I said: 'Don't worry.'

She said: 'Call Fakhri to bring me something to put over my shoulders.'

And she began to cough. I spoke to Fakhri and also said: 'If Madame says something, make sure it doesn't slip your mind or you'll . . .' and I pinched her lips and gave her a squeeze. I said:

'Laugh! Cackle away!'

She said: 'But Madame . . .'

I said: 'It's fine. I want her to hear you.'

And there, right there on the landing . . . She said: 'Not here, it's not right, Prince.'

I said: 'And why not?'

She said: 'Well, it's cold. My back is freezing.'

I said: 'With all this flesh, what have you got to worry about? Laugh, girl, nice and loud! And if Fakhronissa asks, "Why were you laughing?" just say the Prince told you to. Don't be afraid. Just say it. But don't forget that you are going to have to tell me how she takes it, when you tell her, her eyes, her hands, down to her lips.'

Fakhronissa had said: 'You're a good girl, Fakhri love.' And she had smiled and dug her hands into the pockets of her coat. Her eyes behind her spectacles would not have flickered. Fakhri kneels down before her and says: 'Madame, by God I . . .' She says: 'I know. You're a good girl.' She strokes back the hair from Fakhri's forehead. She'd done up the collar on Fakhri's dress. Then she said: 'Fakhri, go to the bathhouse. It's not right carrying on like this. A whole week that you . . .'* She says: 'Actually, Ma'am, I have the curse. When it's over, I promise.' Fakhronissa says: 'What! How can the Prince, at times when you . . .' Fakhri sobs and lays her head in Fakhronissa's lap. And Fakhronissa strokes Fakhri's hair. She'd said: 'You're a good girl, Fakhri.' And she had coughed.

As I came down the stairs I saw that Fakhri had her by the shoulders. Fakhronissa was still coughing. She said: 'Prince, if you have a moment, would you call on Dr Abu Nuvas and tell him to come.' I said: 'We have a

* In the old days in Iran, it was the custom of women to visit the bathhouse after making love. In one of Mahasti's quatrains, a couple are so fond of each other that the entire town runs out of water.

telephone. Tell Fakhri to call him.' She said: 'Look, Khosrow Khan, it's nothing to do with me, but wouldn't it have been better not to have sold the tulip lights? At least you might have left them for me.' I said: 'We haven't room for all this junk.' She said: 'Should we wait up for you tonight?' I said: 'I don't know. Let's see what happens.' Fakhri had her head down.

That night when I got home, I heard Fakhronissa's voice upstairs. Fakhri said:

'The doctor came. He said: "Madame, in your condition you should not be drinking wine. Or at least you should cut down." Fakhronissa said: "Sooner or later . . ."'

I said: 'Fakhri, tell me about the morning.'

She told me.

I said: 'When you went upstairs, what happened?'

She said: 'Madame was lying on her bed. She said: "Fakhri, why can't you laugh properly?" I wanted to say: "You see, Ma'am, the Prince tickles me with a feather." But I didn't. Madame said: "I know, but what I can't understand is how the Prince can do it with you when you have the curse."'

I said: 'What else did she say?'

She said she didn't know, that she'd forgotten, that she didn't like to say . . . So I slapped her on the face. She said: 'I think she said . . .' She began to cry and said: 'Please, I can't remember every last thing.'

On the bed, and all around the plasterwork and the chandelier in the middle of the ceiling and the mirrors inlaid in the plasterwork and the books . . . From the bed one can't see oneself in all that mirror work. Munireh Khatun, she would have managed.

The doctor comes. Fakhri is there too. The doctor says: 'Madame, we'll need to take a chest X-ray.' Fakhronissa says: 'Just prescribe me a linctus or something that'll stop the coughing, or at least so I can get up on my feet.'

I said: 'What else did they say, Fakhri?'

She said: 'They didn't say much. The doctor left soon afterwards. At the door, he said: "Fakhri, your mistress is very ill indeed. Pass on my respects to the Prince, and tell him that he should please have a thought for his wife, otherwise . . ."'

I said: 'Laugh, Fakhri. Give a good cackle. I can't bear to hear her coughing. Laugh!'

Fakhronissa coughed in the same way as Grandfather and Grandmother. Fakhri would say: 'Please, Prince, one can't laugh just like that.' I used to tickle her with a feather in the armpit or on the soles of her feet. Fakhri used to wriggle. Her breasts wobbled. She used to laugh so much her eyes filled with tears. But then I'd hear the sound of Fakhronissa coughing. I used to bury my head in Fakhri's hair and stop my ears.

And upstairs, on that bed, when she heard Fakhri laugh, amid the plasterwork and the little mirrors, the hangings and the chandelier . . .? The books in the shelves, beside the bed, or above the stove, piled on top of one another. If she had turned her head, she could have seen her bookmark on the table. Was it like that? She never once said: 'You're a good man, Prince.'

I could never persuade her to let me see her naked. She used to say: 'I don't care for it, Prince.' In the dark I'd lie down beside her and run my hands over her whole body. She'd say: 'Hurry up, then leave me in peace. I want to sleep.' But she couldn't get back to sleep. She would say: 'Get up and read me a couple of pages from that book, maybe . . .' I would say: 'You're at it again, Fakhronissa? I'm sleepy.' She'd say: 'Light that lamp, and put it beside you.' I would sit beside her on the bed and read aloud. She would put her hands behind her head and stare at the ceiling while I read. When I glanced at her, she'd say: 'What are you thinking about, Prince?' One of her breasts was showing. The lamplight fell on it. I'd stare at the curve of her lower breast as it passed into shadow. She said: 'Read, Prince.' I must have been drunk because I reached out and undid the button of her night-gown. She was still lying like that, hands under her head, looking at the ceiling. I said: 'I love you, Fakhronissa.' She burst out laughing, so loud that her eyes filled with tears. She didn't have her spectacles on. Fakhri could never laugh so loud and yet so musically. Not in a lifetime. I tried everything, but it was no good. Her big tits would shake, and she would open her mouth so wide I'd see all her teeth. She just couldn't. It was as if she was gargling water. I would hit her, but she still couldn't. I would say:

'Like that, yes, laugh loud.'

I would tickle her under the armpit until she'd be in tears. I would lie down beside her and hide my head in her hair or on her breast. She was warm. I'd lie right there in Fakhri's bed. But I could not get to sleep. Fakhronissa's coughing came in dry bursts.

When they took away the bier and extinguished the lamps and the whole shrine smelled of aloes, and the Koran readers brought the funeral recitation to an end and left, Fakhronissa – without plucking her carnation from the vase and putting it in the corner of her mouth – went back into the photograph frame and sat down. The dust settled on her hair as the Prince watched. And he saw that Fakhronissa, underneath the dust on her hair and the lace dress and the spectacles and the white skin –

way out beyond his reach – both was and was not. And there was the white sheet and blood that was leaking from the corner of Fakhronissa's mouth. And once again he heard the squeak of wheels and Hassani's footsteps. The wheelchair was coming upstairs and Murad was muttering:

'Hurry up, woman.'

Hassani said: 'But I'm exhausted. Do you really need to go up all these stairs?'

Then there was just the rolling of the wheels on the tiles of the hall. As the door opened, the Prince could hear only the sound of the wheels and the woman's footsteps. The door was closed.

'Greetings.'

'Greetings,' said Hassani, too.

The Prince said: 'Murad, so it's you again. Haven't I told you a hundred times . . .?'

The Prince sensed only the gentle progress of the wheels over the carpet. Mice were gnawing away at something. The Prince cried out:

'Murad, has somebody died, eh?'

And he coughed. A match was struck and the Prince glimpsed just those two eyes in a maze of wrinkles and the faint light of the tip of a cigarette. He knew that by now the wheelchair was by the stove and Hassani was raking through the ash for something. He heard again the sound of mice gnawing. A long bout of dry coughing shook the Prince's shoulders.

Murad said: 'Dear Prince, Prince Ehtejab has passed away.'

'Ehtejab?' the Prince asked.

Murad said: 'Don't you know him? The son of Colonel Ehtejab, the grandson of the Great Prince, the great-grandson of His Most Glorious and Illustrious Majesty. I mean Khosrow, who as a boy on ceremonial days used to stand beside the Great Prince who would pass a hand over his hair and say: "My boy, don't turn out a pimp like your father."'

The Prince said: 'Aha.'

'He had T.B., was thin as a spindle, you couldn't recognise him. May God have mercy on him.'

A cough shook the Prince's shoulders. And the Prince heard the coloured-glass windows rattle, and the chandeliers and the dishes on the shelves and the photographs of Grandfather and of Grandmother, Father and Mother, paternal aunts and even the picture of Fakhronissa. And the Prince saw Fakhronissa stretched out under the white sheet and blood leaking through the sheet and spreading wider and wider. He coughed up blood into his mouth and on his lips.

The mice had gone. The Prince's head was bowed, resting on his shuddering hands. His forehead was cold. A false dawn lit the room and from the outskirts of town the cocks were crowing. The Prince heard dogs barking and the sound of wheels rolling over the carpet and then the door opening and shutting again. The wheels squeaked on the hall tiles and on the steps. Murad said:

'Move, woman!'

And Hassani said: 'But I'm tired. Do you really have to go down all these stairs?'

The stairs were damp and they had no end. And the Prince who knew that he was not capable, that Grandfather had overwhelmed him, that Fakhronissa . . . Down all those steps he went, down and down all those steps that led to those dank passages and that icy vault and the sheet and the blood and the staring eyes that both were and were not.

FINIS